DIABLO

Part Five of the Sistema Series

A DYSTOPIAN HORROR

ULTAN BANAN

Cover design by Ultan Banan © 2025
Editing by Seminal Edits

ultanbanan.com

ISBN: 978-1-914147-33-3

DIABLO

I

The entrance to the basement bar was nestled between a Pink Milk dispensary and a Virtual Junkie parlor, in the back-quarter Mercantile where black-market chopshops and seedy eateries ranged the alley like broken teeth, where sparks rained down from the stitched canvas of overhead pirated electricity cables, the air heavy with the stink of roasting pork. The bar was ignored or unnoticed by those not seeking it out; above the door a sign, long on the blink, might have read 'DEEP', or 'DEEPER'. Behind the black aluminum door, half open and dented with a thousand kicks and drunken blows, jagged stairs ran down to the sub-level dive below.

The air inside was rank with the hum of degeneracy. A thin trail of smoke draped the low ceiling of the place, and the floor was dappled with jagged pebbles of broken glass and bore the stains of a myriad dirty nights.

A hefty barman stood rubbing a glass with a dirty rag. A blue bandana covered his pate, his sleeveless vest showing inked upper arms and the low cut of it exposing a hirsute gut. He tweaked the rag and the glass in opposing twists as he looked out over the listless bar, eyes stopping to appraise his derelict clientele with a bored lechery.

When the glass squeaked dry he put it top-down on the bar, flicked his dirty rag over his shoulder and gazed at a teenage boy seated at a table by the door, next to him a man well on in years who had the look of a jaded teacher. The barman poked a fat finger into his belly button and scratched. A scrawny little faggot sitting at the bar watched the barman, gazed longingly at the finger exploring the depths of the hairy cleft; the faggot raised a highball to his lips but didn't drink, merely let his tongue rove over his upper lip as he twitched in his seat, his eyes locked on a scene he, in his mild drunkenness, longed to be a part of.

'Lend a hand?' he muttered, his eyes rising to the barman's, locking on, as the barman turned from the fairy by the door, realizing he himself was being scrutinized.

The barman's eyes took a second to refocus. He pulled away from whatever scene he was playing in his mind, and when he'd appraised the desperate queer at the bar, he merely grinned then turned away disinterestedly. Whether inadvertently or by design the barman bent over, exposing the crack of his fat ass to the queer, who gulped the drink in his hand ravenously sending streams of it down his chin and onto his white vest.

In the corner of the room, sitting at a table alone, a man watched.

In the clammy heat the man looked hot, sweaty even, yet the bottle in front of him sat untouched. As he looked at the scrawny faggot at the bar, his tongue flicked over his lower lip before he caught himself and turned to scan the room. He sat unnoticed. Finally the man turned to his beer, lifted it and raised it to his mouth and sank it in one. He put the bottle down.

When he turned back to the bar, the faggot was watching him, his eyelids half-closed in drunkenness.

The man burped. First alert at finding eyes on him, he relaxed, turning his body to face the queer at the bar. He wiped his mouth with the palm of his hand then lifted the hem of his shirt, sliding a hand onto his belly. The queer's eyes followed the movement.

With only a moment's hesitation, the queer slid off his seat, glass in hand, and crossed the grimy floor. He stopped at the table for a second, and when the man in the corner didn't object, slid into the booth opposite him.

They sat in silence for a moment. A flash of disdain crossed the man's eyes before his eyelids narrowed and he surveyed the youth in front of him with a kind of hostile curiosity, the youth excited by the violent tension.

The queer looked at the empty bottle in front of the man. 'Wan' another?'

The man shook his head, taking his hands from where they rested on his gut and placing them on the table. The youth caught the flash of the wedding ring, noted it, his eyebrow rising. He put his glass to his lips and drank. His eyes were glassy with drunkenness, but they didn't break contact with the man's as he took a gulp. Then he put the glass down.

Edgy now, he was compelled to break the tension. 'So... what are you into?'

The man shrugged. He stared intensely at the queer. Then he reached out and picked up the highball, raised it to his lips and spat into whatever was left of the cocktail. He held it out.

The queer's eyes narrowed. He stared at the glass. Then he raised his eyes to the man as he scratched his cheek. After a moment's pause, he grinned. He took the glass, put it to his lips and swallowed. The man nodded. Then he shrugged.

'After you,' he said, tilting his head in the direction of the toilets.

The queer gave the man a final appraisal, then gave an imperceptible drunken nod. He put down the glass and slid from the booth, turning on his heels, eyes still on the man. He sauntered toward the toilet doors. The man slid from the booth and followed.

The toilets were graffitied and rank with neglect. High up on the wall a cracked hopper window opened onto the alley at the back. A flickering bulb tinkled with a halogen rattle. The two of them were alone.

The queer entered and paused at the entrance to a stall, looking half over his shoulder for the man to come in after. When the toilet door swung open, the man paused in the doorway and looked at his prey; the queer's eyes dropped to the man's pants, where the bulge of an erection was already apparent. The queer's tongue flicked over his lips. He entered the stall. Seconds later, the man followed. He closed the door.

The queer leaned back against the wall and began to pull his vest from his pants. The man shook his head.

'Get down on your knees, faggot,' he uttered, the croak of lust in his voice.

The queer's mouth opened obscenely as he slid to his knees. The man took hold of his belt and undid his pants. Then he took the queer by the face and slapped him, and reached into his pants.

'I got what you want, you filthy fuck…'

The man went at the faggot for all of a minute, and when he was done, he tucked his cock away and leaned back against the wall, panting and spent. The queer wiped his face, leaned his head back against the wall and closed his eyes, face raised to the ceiling.

'It's not enough,' he whispered. 'I want more…'

The man grinned. His tongue protruded from his mouth, hanging there grossly for a second. Then he closed his fly and did up his belt.

He wrenched open his tie, pulling it over his head and stuffing it in his jacket pocket. He opened his shirt to expose a corpulent, hirsute belly.

'You want more, huh? I got more for you… come here.'

The queer grinned then slid forward on his knees and put his hands on the man's belly. He put his cheek against the hairy gut and began to rub his face all over, then he began licking. The man spread his belly button.

'Get your tongue in there, faggot…'

The queer pushed his tongue into the man's navel and began to tongue it grossly.

'There you fucking go...'

The queer was lost in the filthy act when a sudden start from the man's stomach – as if something inside was trying to push its way out – caused him to flinch and pull back.

He stared at the stomach for a second in incomprehension. 'What the fuck is that?'

The man shook his head. 'Ain't nothin' to worry about.'

The queer looked up at the man then back at his belly, and was just leaning in to get going again when there was another, this time more violent. The queer recoiled back against the wall.

'Yo, what the fuck...?'

The man took a step forward. He looked down at the queer. 'I got babies.'

The scrawny teen's forehead creased. 'You what?'

'They're my babies.' The side of his lips raised. 'Wanna see?'

The man took the queer by the throat and pinned him against the wall. The queer's eyes bulged and he began to kick, one leg flailing out uselessly. The man began to heave, his stomach and throat contracting as if trying to expel something from deep within. A lizard-like flicker came over his eyes. The queer, sober now in an instant, gawked up at the man in horror.

The man's face went red, bulged. 'I got these things, see...' He gagged, then recovered. 'They're like my... children.' Black bile dribbled from his mouth onto the queer's face. 'And when they want out, they just... want out. I gift one, to you...'

The tail end of a thick black slug wriggled out of the man's mouth. The man's eyes were black now and his face swollen and red. The thing being expelled from him twisted violently as the queer tried to shake himself free, twisting his shoulders and lashing out with two scrawny arms. But the man was too powerful. The fat black slug slithered from the man's throat as he leaned in, and when he was close enough it forced its writhing head between the queer's lips. The queer fought to pull away, but it was no use. The tail end of the slug slipped from the man's mouth and fell with a slap onto its victim's face, and in a second pushed itself into his mouth as his body bucked, the neck muscles straining like taut rope. His throat stretched as the great black thing pushed its way down his gullet.

The queer twisted and spasmed, then in a moment became still. His eyes flashed black, and his body went limp and fell back against the wall of the stall.

The man hovered over the prone form. He reached down and took the queer's face in his hands, and stared into two black eyes.

'Take this gift and be one with it.'

2

The key rattled in the lock and the door opened and Maynes stepped inside. The sounds in the dull suburban home were of children, and beyond that, the rattle of pots from the kitchen.

'Daddy!'

Alerted by the sound of the slamming door, two small children ran from the living room into the hall, and stopped dead, and looked at their father with a kind of awe, and not a small touch of fear. The boy pulled nervously at the seat of his pants; the girl put a finger in her mouth and chewed on it.

'Bah!' Maynes made a mock scare sound and threw his hands out toward the children, eliciting a cry from both. They turned and ran, and Maynes followed them into the kitchen where the children were pressed into their mother for safety, each clasping a thigh.

'What's Daddy doing to you, huh?'

The woman turned as Maynes stepped across the threshold. There was a brief flash of reproach in her eyes, then it was replaced by something like mistrust. She turned back to the counter where she worked.

'I expected you earlier.'

'Something came up.'

The woman went to the fridge, opened it and took out a block of cheese. Maynes, stepping across the floor, reached into the door of the fridge and lifted out a bottle of milk. As he did, the woman's nose twitched, and she leaned in almost imperceptibly in the direction of her husband. If Maynes noticed, he didn't let on.

The woman stepped back and looked at the carton in his hand, then up at him.

'*Milk?*'

Maynes shrugged. 'What? I feel like a glass of milk.'

The woman looked at him for a long second, then tilted her head, her eyes wide in surprise. 'Okay.'

She turned back to the counter as Maynes opened the carton of milk and put his nose to it then raised it to his mouth. The two children watched in silent awe, mouths open, as their father tilted the carton and poured the milk into his open mouth. His wife did not turn, only tilted her head to catch him out of the side of her eye. She picked up a head of lettuce.

Maynes kept drinking until the carton was empty. He let out a gasp after he'd swallowed the last gulp. A trickle of milk ran down his chin and dripped onto his ruffled tie. The two children shared a look at each other then turned back to their father.

The woman turned around, the lettuce clasped tight in her hand. She gave her husband an accusatory glare.

'But you don't even like milk.' She held the lettuce aloft, as if summoning an oracle. 'Since when do you like milk?'

Maynes stood on the pedal of the bin and dropped the carton inside. The bin closed with an aluminum clatter.

He shrugged again. 'I felt like some milk.'

His wife stared at him for a long time, lettuce still in the air. He held her gaze, then he seemed to grow bored. He looked down at the children before growling and making as if to advance on them again. The children turned and ran out from under his grasp, making for the table. The woman pointed the lettuce in the direction of the table.

'Go and sit down.'

Maynes nodded and ambled past her, taking off his jacket.

Her nose twitched again as he passed. Maynes hung his jacket on the back of the door then took a seat across from the two children, who still stared at their father as if at a museum exhibit.

'I'm hungry,' said the little boy, putting a finger in his mouth in imitation of his sister.

'Me too,' said Maynes. He loosened his tie. 'I'm so hungry I could eat a little boy.' He picked up a fork and made as if to fork the boy. The boy recoiled and squealed.

'Maddox…' His wife spoke his name and raised an eyebrow reproachfully.

He put down the fork. 'Let's be good for your mommy.' He winked at the boy.

His wife regarded his face intently before her gaze fell to the milk stain on his tie, lingering there until he turned a hard eye upon her. She looked away.

After dinner, the woman cleared the table and took the children upstairs. Maynes sat in silence at the table. He looked down at his tie where the milk stain had now dried and whitened. He began to pick at it with a fingernail then thought better of it and left it alone. He flattened the tie with his hand. Then he burped, a gurgling sound issuing from his throat, and a contraction shaking him as if something might come up from his insides. His eyes seemed to blacken for a second before their dull brown hue returned. Maynes let his tongue hang from his mouth as he sat there with his hands in his lap. He looked up at the ceiling, where right above his head burned several recessed halogen downlights. He squinted. Getting up, he went to the wall and flicked the switch, the kitchen going dark but for the lights in the vent hood above the oven. He sat back down.

When his wife returned, she stopped on the threshold and looked around the kitchen, then at him. He was sitting, eyes closed, face raised to the ceiling. She reached for the light switch.

He replied without opening his eyes. 'Leave it.'

There was a moment's silence.

'Maddox, I have the cleaning up to do, and I'm not doing it in the dar—'

'Marjorie.'

There was enough weight in his pronouncement that she dropped her hand from the switch, letting it fall to her side before she clutched her skirt and crumpled it in her hand.

'I'll just work in the dark then, will I…'

Her voice didn't have the conviction it had earlier. Marjorie moved to the counter and began to clear it, picking up dishes and packing them into the dishwasher. Maynes sat with his eyes closed. He didn't say anything. Even above the clattering of dishes and cutlery, his breathing was heavy and labored.

As the woman worked, the clattering of dishes into the dishwasher grew louder and more frantic. Eventually Maynes opened his eyes, looking directly at his wife. She didn't turn in his direction, going instead to the sink where she turned on the water.

'Kids in bed?' he offered.

She nodded and muttered a reply in the positive.

'Maybe I'll go up and see them to sleep.'

'Maybe you just leave them be.'

His eyes narrowed. 'Huh?'

'I said, maybe you just leave them be. They've been… wary of you of late. I don't know what's going on with you, but the kids are *wary* of you. I say 'wary', maybe I'm being diplomatic. Sometimes you downright frighten them. Sometimes you frighten me too.'

She said all this without looking at him. Maynes didn't take his eyes off her.

'You're being silly.'

She said nothing. Turning off the tap when the sink had filled with water, she lifted a glass and began to wash it, twisting the cloth with more aggravation than was necessary. When it was clean, she placed it on the drainer and picked up another.

'I said you're being silly.'

She stopped what she was doing and turned to look at him. 'Am I?' She shook her head and began scrubbing the glass. 'Just what's gotten into you, I don't know… I mean, when did you start drinking milk, for instance?'

'Jesus Christ…' Maynes looked down at the stain on his tie, smoothing it once more. 'Again with the milk – who gives a shit about milk? I mean, really, Marjorie… who really gives a shit about milk?'

She looked at him pointedly. 'Don't raise your voice at me.' She put the glass down. 'It's not even about milk. It's about you, acting strange and unusual, and creepy. I mean, why do I come down the stairs at night and find you sitting in the dark, eyes rolling in your head and tongue hanging out of your mouth like some demented fish? I mean, why? And since when do you lock the door when you use our bathroom? Tell me… since when?'

She held the washcloth out at him accusingly. Maynes let his tongue fall for his mouth for a second, taunting her with the gross, pendulous organ. She stared at him in incredulity. Then she shook her head.

'I… cannot…'

She didn't finish the sentence. She placed her two hands on the sink and dropped her head, closing her eyes. She shuddered.

'I'll go say goodnight to the kids.'

He got up from the table.

That night, Maynes opened his eyes and sat up in the single bed in which he lay. It was dark out. Faint light filtered in through the curtains from the streetlights outside and he caught the trace of his reflection in the mirror on the wall opposite. He regarded himself for a moment then turned, pushing his legs from beneath the duvet and setting his feet on the floor. He stood up.

He teetered for a moment before trudging drunk with

sleep to the door. He opened it and stepped into the hall, and crossed the hall to the bathroom, pausing to look over his shoulder at the door to their shared bedroom that they no longer shared. Then he went into the bathroom and locked the door. He didn't turn the light on but stood in the darkness. Leaning back against the cool tiles of the bathroom wall, he closed his eyes and inhaled deeply. He slid his hands under his T-shirt and rubbed his torso, clutching at the loose folds of fat on his ample frame.

Maynes took off his T-shirt and dropped it on the floor. He began to scratch at his skin, fingernails digging deep, pulling at his flesh until thick red welts appeared on his torso. His face contorted and a kind of weeping ensued, a weeping devoid of tears, his face twitching in spasmodic ecstasy.

Dressed in only his underpants, he put his hands on the edge of the bath and climbed in, and lay down on his back. He choked once, spitting a big glob of black bile onto his chest. He rubbed it into his skin and over his belly, before another shot from his throat. Maynes gagged, his throat constricting, as one of the fat black worms pushed from his throat and plopped down onto his chest, squirming in a thick black placenta. Followed another, and another. Soon there were half a dozen of these fat, twitching lungworms slithering over his face and body. Enveloped in their thick sludge, Maynes writhed in a kind of ecstatic stupor. He opened his eyes to the ceiling. The black of endless night was in them.

3

Maynes looked up as the lift doors opened to see two men in stiff black suits waiting in the foyer. His eyes narrowed. He looked from one to the other before he stepped out. He paused in front of them, issuing a sigh of impatience.

'What is it?'

Melville, a shifty-looking security underling, cleared his throat. 'Rodin needs you to come downstairs. Follow us, please.'

Maynes made no movement. 'Can't this wait til after lunch?'

'It's a matter of some urgency, sir. We need you to come with us right away.'

Maynes looked from Melville to his partner, du Pont, who remained silent. Du Pont kept his eyes on Maynes, a look of hostility on his face. Maynes's look was none too cordial either. His lip twitched momentarily into a snarl of aggression before righting itself. Then he pulled on the lapels of his jacket, glanced at the ceiling quickly then gave a conciliatory flick of the head.

'Come on, then.'

'Sir.'

Melville and du Pont turned. Maynes followed.

Maynes caught sight of Rodin ensconced at his desk as

the three entered the Security wing. When Melville stopped to knock on the door, Rodin didn't look up, so engaged was he with the screen he pored over. Melville knocked a second time. Rodin raised his face to the door, then lifted a hand and waved them in. Melville opened the door and stepped inside. The others followed.

Rodin nodded a greeting to his fellow head of department. 'Maynes.'

Maynes reciprocated. 'Rodin.'

Rodin looked at the two grunts and tilted a head toward the door. Melville followed du Pont out, where they took up a standing position back against the wall on the other side of the corridor. Maynes glanced at them over his shoulder before turning back to Rodin.

'We got a problem here?'

Rodin shrugged mysteriously. 'I dunno. I hope not. But that's what we're here to find out. The sensors went off as you were riding up in the lift this morning. Naturally we got to check it out.' He stared at Maynes pointedly.

'The sensors?'

Rodin nodded. 'A foreign body was detected. Now, false alarms are known to happen, but they're extremely rare. We're gonna have to put you through the body scanner, but before we do, I need to ask you a few questions.'

'The scanner?' Maynes's shoulders drew up defensively.

'The scanner. Now, bear with me...' Rodin punched a key on the keyboard, his attention turning to the screen in front of him. 'So... Have you had any unsanctioned medical procedures since you were last at work?'

'No.' Maynes lifted his face to stare at the blank wall behind Rodin.

'No laser eye surgery or hearing procedures?'

'No.'

'Have you had any unsanctioned hardware adjustments made to your work phone?'

'No.'

'New software installed?'

'No.'

'Were you asked by any third parties to carry unsanctioned materials into work today?'

'No.'

'Any new piercings or tattoos?'

Maynes shook his head in impatience. 'No.'

'Have you had any concerning encounters with needles in the past twenty-four hours?'

'I have not.'

'Have you smoked, inhaled or injected any illicit substances?'

'No I have not.'

Rodin looked up from the computer screen to scrutinize Maynes's face. Maynes was compelled to meet his gaze.

'Well then. A body scan shouldn't present any issues, but it's a formality we have to contend with all the same.'

'Is it?'

'Yes it is.' Rodin paused for a second, staring at Maynes before putting his hands on the desk and pushing himself up. 'Follow me then.'

Rodin led Maynes outside, where with a word he dispatched Melville and du Pont before leading Maynes down the hall to the assessment room. Inside, a single assistant stood prepping the body scanner. She looked up as the two men entered. Maynes recognized her as the attendant on duty after they'd pulled Zervas from the Inferno program. He hadn't realized she was Security. She glanced at him briefly before turning back to the scanner to make some unknown adjustment.

'All very routine,' Rodin said. 'I'm sure you've had the pleasure before.'

'I have not,' Maynes replied.

Rodin raised an eyebrow. 'Oh? Well then. This'll be an experience for you. Just take your jacket off and make sure you remove all metals – watch, rings – from your person.' He looked at Maynes's waist. 'Belt too.'

Maynes took off his jewelry and dropped it into a tray on the counter, then took off his jacket, folded it, and placed it on the tray. He took off his belt, rolled it up, and placed it on the jacket.

'Just like going through the airport used to be, huh…'

Rodin clacked. 'Just like that, Maynes. Not so long ago now, huh…'

Maynes turned around. He looked at the scanner for a second, the large, imposing piece of equipment also reminiscent of airports of the past.

Then he took a step toward it. As he did, he froze suddenly, his hand going to his gut, which seemed to contract under his shirt.

Maynes's face went red. 'Oh Jesus…'

Rodin's eyes narrowed. 'You alright?'

'No, I'm not alright…' He looked around him. 'I really need a fucking toilet.'

'Right now?'

Maynes hissed. 'Oh yeah… right fucking now.'

Rodin pointed across the room. 'There's one right there. But I would suggest—'

Before he could finish, Maynes turned and hustled for the door, bent over and wheezing painfully. Once inside, the door slammed shut. Rodin turned to look at Diane Cho, a security analyst, who raised an eyebrow. Rodin cleared his throat, shook his head and turned to the machine.

'What parameters have you set it for?'

Diane lifted a clipboard. 'Standard intrusion settings. Want me to tweak it?'

Rodin bit his lip as he stared at the floor for a second. 'Soften the parameters on biomass and heavy metals. By ten percent.' He paused. 'Make it fifteen.'

Diane nodded and went to a computer on the desk, bringing up the operating program and making the necessary adjustments. When she was done, she turned to Rodin and nodded.

Across the room, they heard the bathroom door open. Maynes emerged, his face damp and the collar of his shirt wet.

Rodin folded his arms. 'Everything alright, Maynes?'

Maynes laughed nervously and waved a hand. 'You know, even after fifteen years' marriage my wife's cooking never gets any easier to digest.'

Rodin smiled weakly. Diane turned back to the computer. Then Rodin gestured to the scanner. 'If you're ready.'

Maynes rubbed his belly then sighed. He stepped into the machine. Rodin watched him take position.

'Feet on the imprints on the floor please, and arms slightly parted from your side. That's it... now just look straight ahead.'

He stepped away from the machine as it began to whirr. Maynes stared at the white wall in front of him. The muscles in his neck tensed before loosening again. His fingers coiled into fists.

The scanner's two gyroscopic arms began to move, slowly at first but picking up speed, until they were rotating in smooth circles around the test subject.

'How long's this damned thing take?' he muttered.

Rodin, his back now to Maynes as he looked over Diane's shoulder at the diagnostics, didn't reply.

'Well... everything looking okay, doc?' Maynes said.

Rodin held up a hand. 'Just be quiet for a moment, Maynes. We need all those internal organs absolutely still. Just hold it...'

Maynes cleared his throat, then went silent. Rodin and Diane made no sound as they analyzed the scan's output.

Then Rodin turned around. 'Nothing's jumping out at me, but there're some unusual electrical signals spiking here and there. You're not on heart medication, sure you're not?'

'No.'

'No beta blockers, anything like that?'

Maynes turned his head to look at Rodin. 'I wouldn't be

working here if I was. You know that.'

'Yeah. Sure.' Rodin nodded once and turned back to the screen. 'How long's that?' he said quietly to Diane.

'Almost a minute.'

'Okay. Wind it down.'

After a few seconds the gyroscopic arms slowed, finally coming to rest. Maynes relaxed his taut body and sighed.

'Am I good to get out of this thing?'

'Out you get,' Rodin replied, folding his arms. 'That'll do for now.'

Maynes picked up his wedding ring and put it on, before slipping on his watch and clasping it. After putting on his belt, he picked up his jacket. 'I take it everything is good?'

Rodin shrugged. 'Nothing out of the ordinary. Some strange electricals, as I said. A full report will be printed up and sent upstairs.'

Maynes nodded. 'Of course.'

'You'll hear from him. Not me.'

Maynes slipped on his jacket. 'I hear ya. We done here?'

'We're done, Maynes.' Rodin opened a cupboard above the counter and took out a tub, unscrewing the lid and holding the tub out to Maynes. 'Need a lollipop, big boy?'

'Fuck you.'

Maynes went out.

Emerson was engaged in a strange contortion when Maynes walked through the door. His arm was twisted around his back and reaching up under his jacket. It took Maynes a moment to process, then he realized his boss was trying to scratch himself. Emerson turned from the viewing window, regarded Maynes for a moment, then his eyes went to the desk in the center of the room.

'Jesus H. Christ – pass me that pointer, will ya?'

Maynes turned to see what Emerson was indicating, seeing the pointing stick on the desk. He picked it up, walked around the desk and handed it to Emerson.

'Gimme that thing…'

He snatched it out of Maynes's hand and flicked it, the thing extending to twice its length. Then he reached around and pushed it under his jacket and began to vigorously attack the source of his irritation.

'Christ Almighty… that's it, Holy God… I swear, I told my wife to change the washing powder, but she just won't listen. She's got it in her head it's the only one worth having, and she just won't change her mind. I'm sure you can relate, Maynes.'

Maynes nodded. 'Sure can, sir.'

Emerson stopped scratching, struck the pointer, compacting it, then turned around and tossed it at the desk. It skittered across it, stopping short of spilling onto the floor. Emerson turned to look at Maynes. His eyes narrowed as he scrutinized him.

'What's this I hear about you setting off alarms?'

Maynes met his boss's eyes momentarily, before turning to look through the glass into the room beyond. It was an Analytics terminal booth, mostly used for testing new software. In the center, a chair, behind it an operator's terminal. On the wall directly ahead, three screens. The room was empty.

Maynes shook his head. 'I dunno, sir. Could've been anything. Maybe some synthetic fibers found their way onto my clothing. Maybe high iron content in whatever I ate last night. I've no idea. I just been to see Rodin.'

Emerson turned away. 'I heard. Seems the report didn't pick anything up. Nothing obvious anyway. Just hope it doesn't happen again.'

'Of course it won't, sir.'

'Yeah. Good.'

He fell silent, gazing through the viewing window to the empty room beyond. Maynes followed the direction of his gaze, as if he might discover the reason for their being there.

'What are we doing, sir?'

Emerson didn't look at him. 'Just wait. We got a few tests to run you might appreciate sitting in on.'

A door opened on the other side of the glass, at the back end of the room, and a sole figure entered.

Maynes raised a hand to scratch his cheek. 'That's Zervas's operator, isn't it?'

'Prestwick, yeah. They call him 'DP'.'

'They putting Zervas under?'

Emerson nodded. 'Gonna run some penetration on him. But to be honest, his mind's like custard. Don't know what we're gonna find.'

Prestwick sat down at the terminal station. He punched a few buttons and the center screen on the wall flickered with static before going black again. Then a door at the opposite end of the room opened. A nurse pushed a wheelchair through the door, in it, Vangelis Zervas. Zervas's chin was slumped down on his chest. Following after them was one of Rodin's security grunts. The nurse stopped in front of the chair and the security grunt lifted Zervas, the medical gown Zervas was wearing hoisting up over his knees. The grunt pivoted and plopped Zervas in the chair without a great deal of care. Then he turned and went out, the nurse swinging the wheelchair about and pushing it out the door after him.

Maynes heard the door behind him open. He turned to see Deen, head of Analytics, come in.

'Come on in,' Emerson said, as Deen closed the door. 'Been waiting to get this show on the road.' Emerson folded his arms as Deen came up beside the two men. When Maynes turned back to the viewing window, Gottfried from Analytics was applying an epidural to the unconscious Zervas.

'So, what's this procedure all about then?' Maynes said, sighing.

Deen glanced at Emerson before speaking. 'It's a digging operation. Inferno so scrambled Zervas's mind that we've been unable to reach him via the framework. We've written a program designed to locate him via a process of transference. Or more accurately, regression.'

'What does that mean exactly, Deen?' Maynes said.

Emerson grunted. 'Yeah, break it down for us old heads.'

Deen shifted the glasses on his face. 'It means we've recreated, to the best of our ability, an environment that replicates a time in Zervas's life when he felt safest.'

'And then?' Maynes raised an eyebrow.

'Well, technically, then, he should just find his way to it.'

Emerson exhaled impatiently. 'We're going fishing, is what you're saying.'

Deen nodded. 'That's about the height of it.'

'Something tells me I'm not gonna like the probabilities on this,' Emerson said.

Deen cleared his throat. 'It's not a perfect set-up, no. But since we're not allowed to resuscitate him, all that remains is to get creative.'

'He hasn't come round since we pulled him out?' Maynes said.

Through the viewing window, Maynes watched Gottfried stick a needle into Zervas's arm and depress the plunger.

'We haven't let him,' Emerson said. 'Deen will explain why.'

Deen took the cue. 'We ascertained that lifting Zervas out of his coma and back into consciousness would prompt him to automatically begin pushing his experiences deep into his subconscious, making it more difficult for us to retrieve any workable information. Therefore, it was safer to keep him under. If we can only find him within the framework, everything we extract will be all the more tangible.'

'Sounds like a shitshow to me,' Emerson muttered.

Maynes loosened his tie. 'Send me in, sir.'

Both men turned to look at him. Emerson glanced at Deen then back at Maynes.

'Say what?'

'Send me in. Get me down there with him. I'll flush him out and into this... neuro-fucking-creche, or whatever it is you've built to find him.'

Emerson turned to Deen. He looked at him without speaking for a second. Deen lifted the pen from the pocket of his lab coat and toyed with it nervously.

'I'm not sur—'

Maynes turned to face the two men. 'Let me do it. Put me in with him. I can find him.'

Emerson didn't look convinced. He turned to Deen. 'Could it work? Would it help, at least?'

Deen hesitated. 'I'm not so… I dunno. We'd have to do some recalibrating, and we'd have to scramble Maynes's signal in some way… but if we could set up Maynes as a kind of polarizing force, driving Zervas toward our safe zone, we might have something to work with.'

'How long's it gonna take to set up?' Emerson said.

Deen shrugged. 'If I put three people on it… two hours, maybe.'

'Do it.' Emerson turned to Maynes. 'You sure you're good for this?'

Maynes nodded. 'Don't worry, sir. I'll flush the fucker out.'

4

Maynes felt the familiar heat shoot up his spine followed by the blinding flash that seemed to sear his brain. When he opened his eyes he was standing in an endless nothingness, darkness in all directions. Under his feet he felt something like ground, but at the same time felt like it might swallow him if he lifted a foot. He touched his body to see if he was clothed; he was not, but a second later there was another blinding flash and he was suddenly standing on a deserted city street, a modern, nondescript concrete jungle, but one from decades past, not the glass-and-steel city he was familiar with. It was the kind of dull district where city began to give way to suburbia, but where bungalows and townhouses had not quite yet appeared. Maynes looked down. He was wearing fatigues and boots, like back in his military days. On his hip was a hunting knife.

Deen's voice came to him.

—Hello, Maynes. Can you hear me?

'Yes.'

—Good. The program you're in is the environment we've created to lure Zervas, and we're right now patching you in to his subconscious feed. Both of you are tethered to the System A framework, so one way or another, one of you is probably going to find the other.

Emerson butted in. —You know there are too many unknowns on this, Maynes. We have to assume time is not on our side – fuck knows, Zervas's heart could stop at any minute on us, so we need you to be quick. Do what you have to do.

'Yes sir.'

—We can't guide you on this one, Deen said. —Our staying in contact with you is only going to create instability in the framework, so we have to go silent.

—Hear that, Maynes? Emerson said. —You're on your own.

'I got it.'

—If anything goes south, you can pull yourself out by jacking the feed. We'll hear you. I'd rather you don't come back empty-handed though.

'I won't, sir. I'll do what I have to do.'

—Good. We're going silent then. Good luck.

—Good luck, Maynes, Deen added.

Maynes heard no more. He turned his head to look up the street, then in the other direction. An eerie tranquility hung over the place, something otherworldly. It was, of course, an artificial reality, but nothing about it appeared unreal. The sky above was the only thing that hinted at something untoward. There was a heaviness, a disturbance in it somehow unnatural.

Maynes took a few steps on the empty street. The buildings around him were low one- and two-story block buildings, interspersed here and there with New England-style commercial units. No life was apparent, either within these buildings or on the street outside. Maynes continued casually up the street, eyes darting all around. Movement to his left caught his eye, and he turned to see a large black German schnauzer come out of a driveway. Catching sight of Maynes, it stopped. Maynes came to a halt, eyes on the dog. After a pause, the large beast padded cautiously out into the street, approaching slowly. It got to about eight feet from Maynes and stopped.

'Come here, pal...' Maynes tapped his thigh, but the dog

came no further. 'Cautious little son of a bitch, aren't ya?'

Maynes rested his hand on his hunting knife.

'Just you here, is it?' Maynes looked around. 'Just you and me.'

Then, as if someone had flicked a switch, a car pulled out of a side street up ahead, followed by another. All of a sudden, the city was populated. Maynes dashed off the road as he heard a car come up behind him.

'Jesus… run right over me, would ya?' He followed the car with his eyes as it sped up the street. When he looked down for the schnauzer, it was gone. He turned and headed up the sidewalk in the direction of *god-knows-where*. But he felt confident, compelled somehow, to follow his instincts.

Ahead he could now see the city proper, Downtown, where skyscrapers rose upward like vast steel turrets, testament to the power of commerce and finance, the twin engines of modern civilization. The skyscrapers were silhouetted against the heavy unnatural sky, the sky stretched like a vast skin over all. Maynes had, for the first time ever, a deep sense that he was intimately linked, an intrinsic part of, this unsettling universe.

He stopped at the curb, waiting for a gap in the traffic. Before he could step into the road, a little voice assailed him.

'You should not be here.'

He turned around. Sitting on the porch of a house on the corner was a little girl. She was barefoot, wore a tattered dress and clutched a raggedy, tired-looking teddy bear to her chest. Her eyes were on Maynes.

'What did you say?'

The girl lowered her forehead, her eyes staying on his. 'I said you should not be here.'

Maynes glowered at her. 'Fuck off, kid.'

He turned away. But the girl did not let up.

'You have a belly full of monsters.'

Maynes started, turning to face the kid. 'The fuck did you say?'

The child stood up and stared him square in the eye. This time, Maynes thought he saw a red glow in her left pupil, as if, behind that eye, some cybernetic mechanism was at work.

The girl suddenly jumped off the step and ran down the side of the house, disappearing through an open picket gate.

'Hey! Come here you little bitch!'

Maynes took a run and leapt over the low hedge and down the side of the house. He barreled through the gate into the back garden, just in time to see the girl disappear through a hole in the hedge. He threw himself after her.

'Little cunt, get back here… I'll pull you limb from limb…'

Maynes leapt through the hedge. The branches tore at his face and arms. He fell through on the other side, finding himself in an alleyway. He looked up to see the girl already halfway up the alley.

'Little bitch,' he whispered. He pushed himself up and took off at a run after her.

The girl took a quick turn at the end of the alleyway. Maynes slipped when he made the turn into the street and stopped himself with a hand on the gravel. When he righted himself, he paused, catching his breath. The girl had disappeared. He followed the direction she'd gone, stopping at the entrance to a court – the only place she could have disappeared into. The entrance to the court was in mission revival style, the gate lying slightly ajar. Maynes stepped inside.

The court was composed of around twelve small bungalows, each with a small patch of grass out the front and connected by an asphalt walkway. Palm trees rose up above the roofs of the small homes, and here and there a potted succulent interrupted the bland run of the courtyard. Maynes scanned about for the child, but she was nowhere to be seen. Hearing the sound of a TV from an open door in one of the bungalows, Maynes stopped at the end of the path. He glanced inside, seeing movement from a kitchen in the back. He took a step forward to get a better look at the figure. It was female, young, back to the door and busy at cooking or some other errand.

He approached the door and stopped in the doorway, and watched the girl, unobserved, for several seconds. The girl, sensing a presence, turned with alarm, but seeing Maynes there, hulking figure in the doorway, her face softened.

'Oh hey there, Mr. Bonheim… I didn't hear you at the door. Do you want to come in?'

The girl was holding a spatula in one hand, the other on the counter. Maynes looked at her in confusion. Her face was warm and open.

'Eh… yeah, sure. I'll come in for a second.'

Maynes stepped into the home, directly into the living area. Next to him was the tired length of the sofa, in front of that a ragged rug, and beyond it an aged television set perched on a vintage cabinet. On the wood paneling of the wall was a large oval mirror, beneath it a cabinet containing an assortment of cheap nicknacks.

The girl turned back to the stove. 'I'm making eggs. You want some eggs?'

Maynes continued through the living area to the kitchen, stopping behind one of four chairs placed around a small table.

'I'm not hungry. I'll take a coffee.'

'A coffee… sure. I'll get you a coffee. Sit yourself down.'

The girl lifted a pot from the stove and began to pour him a cup.

'If you're here to see Mom, she's at work.'

Maynes cleared his throat. 'Uh… that's okay. I'll get her again.'

The girl glanced over her shoulder. 'You're here for the rent, right?'

'Uh, yeah…'

'I know. Mom'll be back at six.'

The girl lifted a pot of sugar, opened it, and dipped in a spoon. She went to dunk it in the mug.

'I don't take sugar,' Maynes said.

The girl looked at him over her shoulder, a curious look on

her face. 'Sure you do, Mr. Bonheim. Black, two sugars.' She gave a pitiful giggle.

When she'd stirred in the sugar, she brought him the cup and put it in front of him.

'There you go, Mr. Bonheim. Can I get you a biscuit or something?'

Maynes shook his head. 'No. Thank you.'

'Right then... oh, shoot!' The girl ran to the stove, lifting the pan from the ring. 'Oh darnit... I almost damned burned them. Oh well...' She fished out the two eggs with a spatula and dropped them onto two bits of toast on a plate, then proceeded to lash them with ketchup. When she'd pulled a knife and fork from a drawer, she brought the plate to the table and set it down. Finally, snatching up a glass of orange juice from the counter, she set it down and sat. She sighed.

'I hate cooking... don't you just hate cooking?' She picked up her fork. 'I mean, I love eating, but I just hate cooking.' Having said it, she cut through a piece of the toast with her fork, speared it, and pushed it into her mouth.

She was a pretty girl if a somewhat awkward teen, with a certain tomboyishness about her. The hair was short, cut around the neckline, and she wore a sleeveless top that hinted at small but perky breasts. She wore a single earring in her left ear and a necklace with a pendant which hung beneath the top and which Maynes could not see.

The girl looked up at him. As if to fill the silence, her words sort of spilled out through a mouthful of eggs.

'Do you like cooking?'

Maynes looked up from her breasts to meet her eyes. 'Um, no, I hate it. I let my wife do all the cooking.'

A look of alarm came over the girl's face. She spoke cautiously. 'Mr Bonheim... but your wife died. Three years ago.' She gave a nervous laugh.

Maynes mirrored her nervous laugh. 'Ah, yeah... that's what I meant... she *used to* do all the cooking.'

'Silly you...'

Maynes nodded. 'Yeah, silly me...' He looked around the room for a family photo, but saw nothing. 'So... where's the rest of 'em?'

The girl swallowed her food and took a slug of her orange juice.

'Well, Mom's at work. Brother's at college.'

Maynes looked to the door then back at the girl. 'Hey, I saw a little girl with a teddy run through here a moment ago... did you see her?'

'What... little Marylou?'

'Yeah... maybe. Remind me what number she lives in?'

The girl shook her head. 'Mr. Bonheim, you sure are acting weird today. You know Marylou doesn't live here. She's in the next court over. She only comes in to steal blueberries off Mrs. Carter's bush.'

Maynes gave a slow nod. 'Oh yeah... yeah, of course.' He shook his head. 'The next court over, I remember.'

The girl laughed nervously again. Picking up her orange juice, she drained it, not taking her eyes off him. She put the glass down.

'You haven't even touched your coffee,' she prodded.

Maynes looked down at the cup, picked it up and took a sip. It was cheap coffee and tasteless, but he put the cup back on the table and smiled nonetheless.

'Very good, thank you.' He pushed back his chair, and pushed himself to his feet. 'Well, I better go and see that this little rascal isn't stripping Mrs. Carter's blueberry bush.'

The girl shook her head. 'You'll never catch Marylou. She's far too fast for you, Mr. Bonheim.' She gave him a sly look. He looked again at her small, pert breasts.

'Well, thank you very much for the coffee, uh...' He paused, feigning forgetfulness. '...Hell, would you believe it, my head is away with it today. I've gone and forgotten your name.'

The girl stopped chewing her food for a second, looking at him with incredulity.

'You really are acting weird today.' She put down her fork

and folded her arms. 'It's Selena.'

Maynes's eyes narrowed. 'Selena…' The name hung on the air for a moment, Maynes's mouth open from the whispered last syllable of her name. He said it again.

The girl raised her eyebrows. 'Uh-huh…'

'Selena Zervas.'

The girl shrugged, as if to say, *Yeah, so?*

Maynes was half-turned to the door but now he turned to face the girl and took a half step back toward the table. She sat back in her chair, unaware what to do with this new tension in the room. Maynes stopped at the wall, where the only photograph hung: a black-and-white landscape of a coastal scene with an island rising from the sea. The picture was imbued with atmosphere; it was of a world that no longer existed.

'Beautiful,' he whispered. The girl did not reply. A shadow darkened the doorway then, and the girl looked up, exclaiming with more relief than she probably intended.

'Vangelis!'

Maynes turned his head to see Zervas in the doorway, silhouetted by the light outside.

Zervas checked on his sister before his eyes flicked to Maynes. The two men stood in silence, regarding each other. Maynes's mouth contorted into a wicked grin.

'Remember me?'

It wasn't clear if Zervas knew who the intruder was, but he treated his presence with suspicion all the same. His eyes dropped to the hunting knife on Maynes's hip. He looked at it for second, then was overtaken by a momentary resolve. Maynes saw it. He made a lunge for the girl just as Zervas propelled himself inside the living room in the direction of his sister. But Maynes was closer. Before Zervas could even get into the kitchen, Maynes had one hand around her throat and the knife at her jugular.

Zervas froze, his eyes locked on his sister. She looked at him in terror.

'Vangelis…' she whispered, her voice trembling.

Zervas held out a hand. 'Just hold on…'

Maynes prodded the blade into her flesh. She gave a whimper.

Zervas gave Maynes a death stare. 'You hurt her, I will cut you into a thousand pieces.'

Maynes chuckled and shook his head. 'Like it even fucking matters here, Zervas.'

Zervas's eyes narrowed. 'How do you know me?'

'Got amnesia, huh? Well, ain't that just fucking swell. Very convenient. I'm a little offended you don't remember me. We were never really pals, but we had a… relationship, of sorts. Not a healthy one.' His grip around the girl's neck tightened.

'Let her go. If you let her go now, I won't kill you.'

Maynes shook his head. 'You don't get it, do you? You're not in control. You've just been lured here, you fucking turncoat. I'm the one in charge. I say what goes.'

Maynes took a half step toward Selena. Maynes, raising the girl's head to expose her neck, tilted the knife as if to draw it across her neck. Zervas froze. Then Maynes thrust her forward, bending her over and smashing her face into the table. She cried out.

With his knife hand he took hold of the back of her pants and thrust them down around her thighs. He looked up at Zervas, a look of pure evil in his black eyes.

'Wanna watch me rape her?'

In a flash Zervas reached down and lifted a cushion from the couch and hurled it across the room. It caught Maynes square in the face. It was enough. In a half second he was across the room; he leapt over the table, crashing into Maynes and sending him thudding against the wall behind. The girl fell, crawling away in the direction of the door. Maynes, winded, found two hands around his throat. The knife was knocked from his hand. He reached up and tried to grab Zervas by the hair but couldn't get a grip. Instead, he thrust a knee up into his balls. Zervas doubled, moaning, but didn't let up his grip on Maynes's throat. Maynes pulled his face in close to his.

'Remember me now?'

He sank his teeth into the flesh of Zervas's cheek and bit down hard. Zervas screamed. Maynes threw him off and clambered on top of him, his hands now around Zervas's throat. He leaned in close.

'Look into these eyes, partner, and tell me you don't know me...'

Zervas looked up into two black eyes, black like two tarry pools, full of malice. Full of evil. He choked, his hands trying to find purchase on Maynes's face.

Maynes gagged, a fat black globule dripping from his mouth onto Zervas's cheek. Zervas's eyes darted about in alarm.

'Let me give you something to remember me by...'

Maynes opened his mouth wide and the tip of a black worm emerged, like a fat, squirming marrow. Before Zervas could react, Maynes pushed both his hands into Zervas's mouth and pulled it open. The worm twisted and pushed itself from its host's mouth, then dropped onto Zervas's face, the head slipping into Zervas's mouth.

Zervas tried to scream. The scream was drowned as if in thick tar.

5

'Jesus Christ, Maynes. What'd you fucking do?'

Maynes came around to the voice of Emerson, the sound a raging cascade spilling into his ear.

'Didn't we tell you not to kill him? He's gone into cardiac arrest, you fucking psychopath.'

Maynes heard the commotion behind him, and looked over his shoulder to see Gottfried hauling Zervas from the chair, overseen by a nurse.

'Quickly,' she prompted, as Gottfried dumped Zervas into a wheelchair. Maynes pulled the epidural from the back of his neck and stood up, and turned around to see Zervas disappear out of the door.

'Wasn't he debriefed?'

'Yes sir,' Deen answered Emerson. 'In full. He was fully aware of the operational risks.'

Emerson turned to glare at Maynes. 'Fuck is wrong with you?' He shook his head. 'I swear to Christ, I'm surrounded by fucking liabilities.'

Maynes protested. 'Sir, I didn't do anything rash. I was just trying to get—'

Emerson held up a hand. 'I don't wanna hear it.' He turned to Deen. 'Get him outta here. Get a report done ASAP. I want to know what the fuck happened.'

'Yes sir.'

Deen looked at Maynes. Maynes knew better than to argue. He turned to follow Deen, but shot a look at Emerson on his way out the door. His eyes seemed to flicker with a black menace.

Emerson's eyes narrowed. 'Don't you give me the eyes, son, I'm fucking warning you. Just you remember the pecking order. I'm top of the chain around here.'

Maynes bit his lip and turned away. Deen opened the door and held it. Maynes marched out. Deen cast a last glance at Emerson.

'Find out exactly what happened,' Emerson said, shaking his head before turning away. 'This whole place is going to shit.'

Maynes stepped out of the lift and into the underground car park and began the short walk to his car. His shirt was in disarray, the collar loose, and the veins in his neck stood out, thick and blue. Sweat beaded his forehead. His tongue flicked out over his lower lip. All of a sudden he stopped, doubling over, hand going to his gut. He grunted in pain, or discomfort. Aware of the cameras in the car park, he stood up straight and forced himself to march the twenty yards to his car. He took out his keys, but fumbled with them and dropped them. He bent down with a groan of pain.

When he slid into the seat and closed the door behind him, he pulled off his tie and threw it on the passenger seat floor. He was about to open his shirt but he stopped, looking out the window around him.

He put on his seatbelt then pushed the key fob, and the car shot to life. He reversed out of the spot and navigated the car to the exit, and waited for the gate to rise. Normally it rose automatically, but this time… this time it didn't. Maynes ducked his head to glance out the window at the camera on the wall above. His palms were sweating. He wiped his mouth with the back of his hand as the other hand tightened about the gear shift. He looked about ready to throw the car into drive, when suddenly a crack of light appeared at the base of the gate. The gate drew up, slowly and with a rumbling mechanical sound. When it was clear of the car, Maynes pushed forward, out of the car park and away from the building.

'Son of a bitch,' he muttered.

He was full-on sweating now.

As soon as he hit the road he sped up, and when he was about a mile clear he pulled off the highway onto a slip road and into the car park of a mostly abandoned strip mall, with nothing still operating but a tired-looking dollar store and a nondescript repair shop. Four boys, young reprobates by the look of it, who were sitting around with a couple of tall boys between them, watched his car pull in and drive past them to the back of the mall, where a couple of burned-out motorhomes sat rotting. Maynes pulled up beside the motorhomes and killed the engine.

'Fuck,' he muttered, scratching at his chest as a prickling heat erupted all over his body. Two beads of sweat pooled and ran down the inside of his eyes and down the ridge of his nose to his lips.

He ripped open his shirt. Red welts had popped up all over his skin, and they were pulsating, as if something beneath the surface was eager to burst out. The welts moved and rippled, each time stretching the skin a little thinner. Maynes gave an animal whimper. Then one, right below his right nipple, burst open. Maynes gave a horrified gasp. First it oozed a few drops of blood, then a small black worm popped half out, wriggling viciously.

'*Ahhh, please, fuck please…*' Maynes whimpered as another one burst out from just above his belly button, and another from his left pectoral. In a matter of seconds, his whole torso was covered in oozing wounds which festered with squirming black worms. They writhed, threatening to leap from his body.

'*Shit, shit…*' Maynes put a hand on the roof of the car, twisting in pain. '*Okay, I'll find someone… I'll find someone.*'

He was about to start up the car again when he glanced in the rearview to see the four boys approaching from the back. He pulled his shirt closed and wiped his face, and glanced in the mirror to check his appearance. He looked crazed.

A tap on the window startled him. He looked up to see the barrel of a gun pointing through the window. The boy holding it tilted his head up, in a gesture the meaning of which could not be misinterpreted. Maynes turned his head to see another boy at the passenger side door. He turned back to the boy with the gun and lowered the window an inch.

'Open the fucking car,' the boy said, flicking the gun.

Maynes nodded. The doors disengaged with a light thump, and simultaneously the four doors of the car opened. The four boys hopped in, slamming the doors behind them. The boy with the gun was directly behind Maynes. Maynes felt the butt of the gun press into his neck. He turned his head to see the boy in front was holding a flick knife. He pressed it into Maynes's torso below his right arm.

The boy with the knife spoke. 'Don't be fucking around now, we just want your wallet.' He paused. 'Fuck it… maybe we'll take the car too.'

One of the boys in the back giggled. They had the cheap stink of beer about them.

The boy with the gun applied pressure to the back of Maynes's neck. 'You heard him – turn over the wallet.'

Maynes looked at the glove box. He tilted his head. 'In there.' He was sweating profusely.

The boy popped open the glove box, rifled around for a second before pulling out the wallet. He opened it and glanced inside.

'Fuckin eh…'

He tossed it over his shoulder to one of the boys in back. Then he took a good look at Maynes. His eyes narrowed.

'Hey, what you hiding under your shirt?'

Maynes didn't answer. He was trembling.

'Hey yo, I think we caught this guy jacking off… hey, you some kind of fucking faggot? You like boys, is that your thing?' The kid glanced over his shoulder at his pal with the gun. 'I think this guy's some old dirty faggot.'

Maynes turned his head to look at the boy. Maynes's eyes flickered with a lizard blackness, making the boy start and retract the knife from his torso.

'What the…?'

Before he could finish, Maynes opened his shirt to reveal the hideous, writhing mass of black worms all over his body. The boy pushed himself back against the window, just as the locks of the car reengaged.

'Jesus *Christ*, what are you?'

One of the boys in the back leaned over for a look then screamed. He turned to open the car door, but when he put his hand on the handle he found several slimy black worms there. He pulled his hand away as they began to crawl up his arm. He screamed again. The boy in front found two on the window next to his head. The boy with the gun was startled by the feeling of something wet crawl up the inside of his calf. The car turned into a thrashing mass of legs and arms, kicking and lashing out. The more they fought, the more of these worms seemed to assail them. Soon they were under shirts, inside underwear, crawling inside ears and mouths. Soon there were so many in the car that they blocked out the light from the windows. As the last scream was choked from the boys, it was as if the inside of the car was drowning in a sea of black bile. A thick black mucus dribbled out of the part-open driver's side window.

Maynes stood outside the car, looking like a man who'd just been dragged out of a cesspit. His open shirt was stained a dark maroon and still damp from whatever his body had secreted. His torso was dark and slimy. His pants clung to him, his hair stuck to his face. He was breathing heavily, and he was barefoot. He stared inside the open door of the car. The car, like something that'd just been dragged out of a river after ten years. Containing nothing but the toxic remains of its once passengers.

Maynes turned to look about him. Apart from the passing cars on the road beyond the deserted strip mall, he could see no one. He scanned the back of the mall, seeing a couple of open doors, others that had simply been kicked in. He walked toward the mall, stopping at the back wall and making his way cautiously along it, passing the first open door and stopping next to the second. He chanced a glance inside. It was the back of the launderette. He heard chatter from the front of the shop, but the back was empty. He nipped inside, quickly scanning the shelves for something he was certain he would find. He came across it on a shelf by the floor – a big box of discarded clothing. Rifling through it he found a shirt and a pair of pants that looked roughly his size. He rolled them up and hurried back out, leaving a slick trail of footprints in his wake.

Before he got dressed he started the car and drove through the fence and out a hundred yards into the scrub beyond the mall car park. He got out, taking the keys but leaving the car doors open. He looked at the gas flap, as if he was contemplating burning the car, but thought better of it. It would only draw more attention. Vathos would have it tracked, and that was a problem. He would just have to come up with a story. Or maybe it was too late for that.

He got dressed, putting on his salvaged clothes and getting back into his shoes. He lifted his jacket, took one last look at the car and turned and marched through the mall car park to the road.

He walked a half mile up the hill and came out right where the Village met Chinatown, and after two hours in a grubby dive bar, Maynes stepped out into a back Chinatown alley. He rubbed his belly through his shirt. He looked down the alley, which alighted onto a small square full of food stalls, full of people. The smells drifting up the alley first made his nose screw up then his gag reflex kick in. He looked like he was gonna throw up but got control of himself. It was enough to make him turn away and head in the other direction, deeper into the seedier parts of Chinatown.

Lights overhead flickered, the occasional flash from an exposed wire somewhere in the great mish-mash of overhead cables, cables that fed every manner of hidden gambling den, backstreet jack joint, soul shebeen, sweat parlor, fuck house, mindwash studio… every manner of decadent and derelict parlor there was going, for pleasure or punishment. Maynes slunked down the alley, guided only by some drunken compass, or perhaps guided rather by the thing that lived inside him.

Compelled by some inner trigger, he stopped at a dubious eatery, no more than a six-square-foot box diner that sold fried food from a tiny window. Next to the window was a tank that displayed the seafood fare. Maynes peered into the tank, looked at the lobster, almost black with a blue sheen to his body, crabs that crawled over the lobster, and a multitude of fat prawn-like crustaceans that nibbled algae off the glass front. It was the eels that caught his attention. Four black eels swimming lugubriously in circles around the tank, eyes so black they were barely visible.

The Asian man behind the counter paid Maynes no attention. Maynes rapped the glass of the window and the man looked up, then he jabbed a finger at the glass tank, rapping on it loudly. Only then did the man open the window begrudgingly.

'Gimme those.' Maynes did a swimming motion with his hand, then held up two fingers. 'Two.'

The Asian man looked at him blankly. 'You wan' fly?'

Maynes shook his head. 'No, no fry. Just give me.'

The man regarded him for a second before donning a black glove. Then he thrust his hand into the tank, fished around for a second before gripping one of the eels by the neck. He whipped it out. Putting it down on a filthy plastic chopping board, he lifted a cleaver. Maynes held up a hand.

'No. Just give me.'

The man paused, cleaver in midair. After a second, he put it down slowly.

'You wan' fish?'

Maynes nodded, holding out his hand. 'Give me fish.'

Slowly, cautiously, the man handed the eel through the window. Maynes took it, gripping it by the neck, holding it aloft in front of him. He looked at it for a second, searching for the eyes. Then he ripped off the head with his teeth and chewed with a thick, rubbery grating noise. Blood spurted from his mouth and dribbled down his chin. The Asian man's eyes widened with something like admiration, the corners of his mouth twitched upward into a smirk. He nodded appreciatively.

Maynes had the eel halfway down him when he rapped the glass of the tank again and held up a single finger this time.

'Wan' more?'

Maynes nodded, pushing the rest of the eel into his mouth as the muscles of the fish spasmed, the tail slapping his cheeks. The last of it was just in his mouth when the man held out the other fish through the window. Before taking it, Maynes took out a wad of dollars from his pocket, fished out a twenty, and put it through the window. The man took it with his free hand and Maynes took the eel.

'Vely good,' the man said, nodding. 'Vely good.'

Maynes turned away from the window, his face slathered with a slimy residue. Two startled and afraid-looking Asian boys, both of them with a cigarette poised at their lips, stood staring at him as he raised the second eel to his lips, bared his teeth, and ripped off the head. The boys gawped open-mouthed at the spectacle before glancing at each other and moving off down the alley, whispering a frantic, hushed Cantonese. Maynes staggered off in the opposite direction, making short work of the remaining eel. When it was finished, he wiped his face with his shirt and continued his demented perambulation.

A small army of men were hosing down the fish market as he passed it, washing rivers of blood and guts into the alley. Maynes waded through the mess, the stench of fish, the metallic stank of blood and bile, coming hard at him as he wandered on. The night was humid and inhospitable. He felt a sudden urge to get off the street.

He stopped in front of a heavy aluminum door. Above the door was a small neon sign the shape of a jack plug. No doubt what the door led to. Maynes held up a fist, paused for a moment, then banged on the door. His mouth open, he looked down at himself as if checking his appearance. He looked up again and banged the door harder. Impatient swearing sounded from the other side, then the door opened a crack. An unshorn face peeked out.

'Fuck do you want, pal?' Maynes looked at this hostile visage for a second, then attempted a glance over the man's shoulder. The man gave an impatient shake of the head. 'I think you've found the wrong place, buddy…'

The man went to close the door but Maynes slapped a hand onto the aluminum.

'I just want a wash, that's all.'

The man glanced him up and down. 'You smell like you need a fuckin' wash n'all, but this isnae the public baths, pal. Maybe you look elsewhere, ya get me?'

He went to close the door. Once again Maynes pushed back. His hand went into his pocket and came out with a wad of notes, maybe two grand.

'Please. I need this.'

The man looked at the cash, bit his lower lip and hissed through his teeth. 'Ah, you pure fucker.' He shook his head. 'I ken by the look of ye you're trouble, partner, I fuckin' know it.' He glanced at the cash again. 'Against my better fucking instincts… Wash, is it?'

Maynes nodded. As if still doubting his decision, the man looked Maynes over once more, holding the door tight. Then he opened it a touch.

'Fuck it. Get ye inside.'

Maynes stepped in and went unsteadily down the stairs.

'I wasn't fuckin' kiddin', pal. Once you're out of here, go get ye a shower,' the man said, shaking his head. 'Some fuckin' folk,' he added, when Maynes was out of earshot.

Maynes proceeded down a short, dark corridor at the bottom of the stairs before entering the basement. It was a standard jack joint, six chairs arranged around the stack, a master terminal off to the side where the chairs were operated from. Three of the chairs were occupied, the others empty.

The man stepped off the stairs and came up in front of Maynes, folded his arms.

'You know exactly what you want?'

Maynes turned from the chairs to look at the man. 'Mind Rotator.'

The man raised an eyebrow. 'You done this before?'

'Yes,' was the reply.

The man tilted his head. 'Alright then. Let's take care of the small matter of payment then we'll get you set up.'

Maynes went into his pocket again and took out the wad. 'How much?'

'All of it.'

Maynes looked up at the man. The man unfolded his arms. He thrust out his chest, pointed a finger at Maynes.

'Lest you've already forgotten, I wasnae gonna let you in. You're pished, and you're filthy. Normally I'd hae closed the door in your face. But you begged me, alright?'

He held out a hand, and after a second Maynes put the whole wad into the man's palm. The man counted it briefly.

'Little short, but fuck it, it'll do.' Then he peeled off a twenty and pushed it into Maynes's shirt pocket. 'Here, for your taxi home.' He pushed the wad of notes into his jeans pocket and pointed at a chair. 'Number two.'

Maynes looked at the other patrons for a moment, seeing the delineations of their respective journeys etched on their faces: one ecstatic, another blissed out. Then he turned and dropped into the chair, putting his hands on the armrests.

The man went to a small fridge and came back with a needle, flicking the hypo with his middle finger and depressing the plunger to send a spurt of liquid into the air.

'Just give me your arm for a second there, pal,' the man said.

Maynes's body tightened and he held up a hand. 'No. No drugs.'

The man sighed and looked at the ceiling, before returning his gaze to Maynes. 'Look, pal, do you know what Mind Rotator is? Because it's not something you do without a little oil in the machinery, you get me? You do this straight, it'll melt your fucking mind.'

Maynes stared at him, his eyes wild. 'I want it raw.'

'Jesus fucking Christ.' The man rolled his eyes, turning away. 'We really got one tonight,' he muttered. Then he turned back to Maynes. 'If you go disco in that chair tonight, pal, I swear tae fuck, I will take you outta here on a gurney and dump you under a bridge, and when you wake up with your mind like fucking spaghetti I will not be there to enlighten the medics as to your predicament, you hear me?'

Maynes nodded. 'I'm no rookie,' he said. 'I want it raw.'

'Fine. Fucking fine.' The man applied an epidural to Maynes's neck, looked at him with something like reproach, then returned to the master terminal. He sat down.

'Right...' He punched a few keys on the keyboard and brought up the operations panel and began to load the program. 'Here ya are then, ya pure fucking bender. Prepare to have yerself a little dram of mind rotation. You wan' it raw, I'll give ye it raw...'

The man punched a button. Maynes's eyes screwed shut. Then his face screwed up and his body bucked, as if delivered of an electric shock. His head flew back against the headrest, the muscles in his neck taut and stretched. His fingers closed like claws over the end of the armrests.

The man swiveled in his chair to look at Maynes. He shook his head. 'Fucking lunatic…'

He watched the contortions of Maynes's body as the program assaulted his mind, the contortions ebbing off here and there as he was taken on a rollercoaster that would shake him to his very subconscious. The man chewed on the fingernail of his little finger as he watched. His knee bounced. He shook his head again, then got up, walking around the circle of six chairs, checking each client in turn, stopping at Maynes to watch his distress. He did another lap of the circle, coming to a stop in front of Maynes once more. A beeping from the master console caught his attention. He turned to look at the monitor, then hurried over and threw himself into the chair.

'No no no…' He punched a few buttons, read the info flashing up on the screen. 'Don't you go veggie on me, ya cunt. We do not like vegetables, ya hear me…'

He scanned the info for a few more seconds. His eyes narrowed and his forehead creased. He got up again, went over to Maynes. Scanned his face. He shook his head.

'I knew you were fucking trouble.' He smacked himself in the side of the head with the ball of his palm. 'When will you ever learn to listen to your gut…'

He was about to turn back to the console when he noticed a sore open up on Maynes's neck. He stopped, looking at it from a distance. Then he moved closer. He leaned in. It looked like a small black worm was working its way out of his neck.

'What in the name of Christ—?'

He didn't finish. A new beeping from the console drew his attention. He spun around and moved to the terminal, putting his hands on the back of his chair. The console flashed with a mass of information. Then he glanced down at the keyboard.

'Sweet lovin' fuck…' he whispered.

A thick black mucus was oozing up between the keys of the

keyboard. Then it came out the edges of the monitor screen. He turned around to see it come through a vent high up on the wall. The man shook his head, his mouth falling open. He felt a feeling overcome him very much like drowning.

6

Maynes heard a noise and opened his eyes. He saw nothing but a blur. He peeled his face from the soft surface on which it rested; he was on a rug. He turned his head to see a fireplace, realizing he was lying on his living room floor. His mouth was dry, and a string of saliva clung from his lip to the rug beneath him. He heard a whispering, and turned to see three figures watching him from the doorway.

'Mommy, what's wrong with Daddy?' a little voice said.

'Shhh,' whispered his wife. Then she pulled the children away. 'Daddy's sleeping.'

Maynes heard the fear in that whisper. The children continued to look at him over their shoulders as they were dragged into the hall. He heard the front door opening and shutting again, quietly, as if they'd all just snuck out. Maynes had a thought.

There's no coming back from this.

He pushed himself up off the floor and stood, shakily, looking at his feet. He had no shoes or socks, and he wondered if he'd come home barefoot. He wiggled his toes. Then he lurched forward and stumbled into the kitchen, his legs going as fast as they would carry him. Over the sink, he slapped his palms onto the counter and threw up, a horrid black and green bile emptying from inside him. Little tiny worms wriggled around inside the mess, but he quickly flushed the sink. He turned away and groaned.

He could smell himself too. It was an alien smell, not something familiar. Something decrepit. He peeled off his shirt, dropped it on the kitchen floor. Then he stepped out of his pants and his underwear. He went out the door into the garage. In the garage he went to the hose and turned on the tap, and began to hose himself down, starting with his face, then his armpits, then finally his balls. When he was dripping wet and rubbed down from head to foot, he turned off the tap.

He felt like an animal.

He noticed for the first time the absence of his car, then the day before came back to him in all its horror. He thought of work, and a lead ball began to grow in his belly. He knew nothing would be the same after today.

Maynes went back into the kitchen, opened the fridge and took out a carton of milk, and drank from the neck the entire carton. He put the carton on the counter and went out, going upstairs and into the bathroom. He stepped into the shower but didn't turn it on. Instead, he stood there for a moment, then bent forward slightly, hands going to his belly. Then he shat himself, watery black shit squirting down the inside of his thighs and pooling around his feet.

He sighed, as if relieved.

'I'll take them all down with me,' he said out loud.

Maynes pulled up in the rental vehicle at the entrance to the underground car park at the Vathos complex, coming to a stop next to an intercom on the wall before the gate. He rolled down the window and waited for the intercom to come to life. When it did, an impatient voice sounded on the other end.

'Yes?'

Maynes tilted his head to send his voice in the direction of the speaker. 'This is Maynes, Maddox, supervising officer of the Subversion department, employee ID 0T277932C. Requesting entry.'

There was a pause. 'Where is your vehicle, Mr. Maynes?'

'I had an accident this morning.'

'This is most irregular. You know protocol regarding the changing of vehicles.'

Maynes sighed. 'Clearly I do. This just happened. I had no time to inform Security.'

'Most irregular.' There was a moment's pause. And then, 'Proceed.'

Maynes watched the gate rise. He waited for it to clear the top of the car then he made his way inside, the gate closing behind him. Parking in his regular spot, he killed the engine and sat for a few moments, his breathing accelerated. He blinked slowly several times then adjusted his tie before getting out of the car and locking it.

At the elevator he stopped, too long, looking at the doors, knowing he was being scrutinized – more so than on any other day – by the camera above his head and the camera on the wall behind him. They would be watching him, he knew it. Perhaps even Rodin himself, watching right this very minute on a monitor over some grunt's shoulder. And now here he was, acting erratically and raising suspicions in management way beyond those he'd already triggered. He reached out and pushed the button. The door opened. He made no move for a second, then finally he stepped in. The doors closed.

He knew what was happening now, could feel it. Just like before, the detectors in the lift were registering alien, foreign bodies in the passenger. Above, in Security, alarms were being triggered. Not something anyone got away with twice.

Maynes felt like the alarms were intimated somehow in his body, as if their warnings were being carried to the molecules of his DNA, which were now oscillating with the awareness. Awareness that they were on to him. That they would be waiting for him.

And they were.

The lift came to stop at the sub-basement level, and when the doors opened, Melville and du Pont were there waiting,

Rodin behind them. The head of Security, waiting just for him.

'Some reception,' Maynes said, stepping out of the lift. 'Should I get used to this?'

'I think you know what has to happen now,' Rodin said. Maynes nodded. 'Why don't you follow us.'

Maynes didn't reply, and when Melville turned and walked down the corridor, Maynes followed, du Pont falling in behind him. Rodin came up the rear.

'Where you taking me?' Maynes asked.

'Somewhere you've never been before,' Rodin answered.

Emerson walked down the hall to the Security wing, scanning his ID card when he arrived at the door. The door opened and he stepped inside, slipping the ID card back into the inside pocket of his jacket. He turned a corner and approached Rodin's office, stopping outside and peering in. Rodin looked up and waved a hand, and Emerson entered, closing the door behind him.

'What's the short of it?' Emerson said, hovering over Rodin's desk.

Rodin rubbed the side of his face roughly. 'He's set off the alarms again. We haven't had him down to Analytics yet – we put him straight in a cell as per protocol.' Rodin punched a button on his keyboard and a screen on the wall came to life. On it, a camera view of a holding cell. Sitting on a short bench against one wall, Maynes.

'What's he doing? How's his behavior been?'

Rodin shrugged. 'Hard to read. He hasn't done much. Walked around for a bit when we first put him in there, then he sat down. He hasn't moved since. That's about an hour.'

'He's been sitting like that for an hour?' Emerson turned to look at Rodin.

'Yep. Hasn't moved. Just staring at the wall, looks like.'

Emerson turned back to the screen, one hand tucked under an armpit while the other slowly scratched his chin. He shook his head.

'We can't bring him down to Analytics, huh…'

'We can,' said Rodin. 'But if he's dangerous… I mean, if he's carrying something, it's risky. That's not a risk I'm willing to take.' He paused. 'You concur?'

Emerson took a deep breath and sighed. He nodded slowly. 'I do. What's procedure? Christ, this has never happened before, not under my watch anyway.'

'Thirty-six hours in the holding cell. We'll notify his wife that he's been held up at work with an emergency. He'll undergo an initial remote interrogation. After thirty-six hours we do a remote scan then a full suite of biochemical analyses. Then the interrogation begins proper.'

Emerson stepped closer to the screen on the wall. He shook his head.

'He also came in in a rental car this morning. Highly unusual,' Rodin said.

'Yeah? Where's his own vehicle?' Emerson said, not turning from the screen.

'We located it immediately. It seems to have been abandoned right off the highway about fifteen minutes from here. Tracker says it's been there since he left work yesterday. We sent a team out about a half hour ago—'

The phone on the desk rang, and Emerson turned from the screen.

'That's probably them now,' Rodin said. He picked up the phone.

'Rodin,' he said, eyes still on Emerson as he spoke. 'You did… uh-huh…' He nodded, then tilted his head enigmatically. 'Right… I'll tell him. We'll be there in twenty minutes.'

He put down the phone.

Emerson held up a hand. 'What – what is it?'

Rodin grimaced and shook his head. 'I don't know, but they said we need to get down there. Immediately.'

The black Suburban pulled into the lot behind the strip mall precisely twelve minutes after leaving the building. Driving was du Pont, next to him in the passenger seat, Rodin. Sitting in the back seat, Emerson, and beside him Gottfried. Already on site were Melville and Merixel from Analytics. The pair stood rather stiffly next to Maynes's car, watching the approaching vehicle. Merixel pulled off a pair of latex gloves and pushed them into her pocket.

The SUV pulled in behind the other Suburban, du Pont killing the engine. Four doors opened and they all stepped out. Emerson slammed his door and buttoned his jacket, and walked toward them silently. His brow was furrowed, and he examined the back of the car as he approached.

'Well?' Rodin said as he came up behind Emerson.

Melville looked at Rodin open-mouthed for a second, then shook his head. 'You're not gonna believe this. This is…' He paused, turning to look in the open door of the car. 'Well, you gotta see it to believe it.'

'What've we got here?' Emerson said to Merixel.

She looked at him. She bit her upper lip; a muscle in her cheek twitched. 'I have no idea what to make of this sir. This is truly messed up. Have a look…'

She pointed in the back seat of the car. Emerson glanced in the open door. The only way to describe it, it was like a car dragged from the river after years underwater. It was slick with a thick black slime, not quite like algae or other underwater growth. It looked like bubbly tar.

'What is that?' Emerson said.

Merixel cleared her throat. 'Sir, we won't know til we get it back to the lab, but it's definitely organic. Probably human.'

'Human?' Emerson croaked. His head shot up. 'This fucking mess?'

Merixel grimaced. 'I wasn't so sure myself. Then I saw this…'

She pointed into the footwell of the car. Emerson crouched, leaning in. He squinted.

'Is that… a *toe*?'

'Yes it is. We've found four already, from at least two different people. God knows what else we'll find when we start digging around in that mess.'

Emerson turned to look at Rodin. Rodin stared at him gravely.

Melville chipped in. 'That thing protruding up next to the toe, that's the melted remains of a Colt .38. There's lots of clothing too. Well, what's left of it.'

Emerson stood up, turning away from the stench. A stench like a cloying hum that seemed to prickle his insides. Merixel pulled a mask from her bag and offered it to Emerson. He waved it away.

'I don't want to see anymore.' He looked around the lot, then over the scrub beyond. Then he turned and looked out to the highway and the city. 'We need to get this out of here, ASAP. Local police aware of this yet?'

'If they were we'd have been alerted,' Rodin said.

Emerson turned to Melville. 'You asked around over there?' he said, pointing to the open back door of a shop in the strip mall.

'I talked to a lady in the launderette,' he replied. 'She said she thought she saw a man nip out the back of the shop yesterday, maybe with a couple items of clothing. But she didn't call it in. She didn't get a good look at him, and anyway, there's nothing there worth stealing.'

'What about the possible bodies?'

Melville held up his hands. 'She says there's usually a group of kids hanging about out here acting like little douchebags, but she hasn't seen them since yesterday.'

Emerson turned back to Rodin. 'Maybe we ask our contacts down at the station about any kids reported missing.'

Rodin was just hanging up the phone. He nodded.

'In the meantime,' Emerson said, 'get a truck down here and get this fucking thing outta here.'

'Just called it in, sir,' Rodin said. 'They're on their way.'

Emerson turned to look at the mess in the car once more, his face a mask of incredulity. 'I've never seen anything like this in my life,' he said. 'Just what in the fuck has he gotten us into?'

7

Emerson looked at the screen on the wall showing the figure of Maynes sitting on the bench. It didn't look like he'd moved. Hands on knees, staring at the wall, his poise was monk-like.

'Tell me that's not sinister,' Emerson said, shaking his head.

'That is highly unusual,' Rodin replied. 'Especially for Maynes. He's not exactly the tranquil type.' He turned to his monitor and punched a few buttons on the keyboard. 'Analytics have the interrogation prepped. Wanna get a start on that or you wanna wait for the initial assessment on the vehicle?'

'We need to wait on the vehicle results,' Emerson said. 'We need a better idea what kind of shit he's unleashed.'

The phone rang. Rodin picked it up. He nodded, said 'Okay', then, 'I'll let him know'. Then he put down the phone.

'That was Medical. It appears Zervas is out of the coma.'

Emerson perked up. 'He's awake?'

Rodin shook his head. 'No, and they don't want to administer any medication in case they induce another cardiac arrest. They're gonna leave him be for now.'

'I'll take a walk up there,' Emerson said, buttoning his jacket.

'Want me to come with you?'

Emerson shook his head. 'Stay here. Stay on top of

the investigation on the vehicle. Let me know when the assessment is ready.'

'Okay.' Rodin stood up and walked Emerson to the door.

Emerson stopped in the hallway and turned to him. 'I've got a feeling we're in for one of those long, horrible fucking nights.' He raised his eyebrows a touch. 'You might be needin' to phone the wife.' He turned and left.

Emerson found Medical empty. The main room was devoid of activity, save for the flickering lights of consoles and the beeping of complex analytical programs displayed on company monitors about the room. Emerson saw the patient Zervas through the glass that separated him from the recovery room. He regarded him, considering the man once a promising asset to the company, an asset for which hundreds of thousands of dollars had been spent on training and development: advanced physical training, cerebral upgrades, cutting-edge psychological and metaconscious coaching, tailored real-life scenarios designed to hone his instincts for the tasks to which he'd be assigned, not to mention all the software which had been developed purely for his own role assimilation. Maybe millions, all counted. And now? His mind *god-knows-how-fucked*, his body hooked up to a dozen different monitors. On the cusp of another cardiac arrest. Dead meat. They were hanging onto him in the hope of gleaning some intel with which they could recalibrate the Inferno program, but whether they'd find anything salvageable, they'd no idea. His mind could be scrambled eggs. And the Inferno program… what a fucking debacle. The program was the brainchild of a very gifted programmer called Ernest Gulliver. A lunatic, but a genius one. He'd worked for the company at the very top level, in a small but somewhat secretive unit that ran alongside but outside the jurisdictions of Analytics and Subversion. Drove Gottfried crazy, knowing all his work was being filtered through to this shady detail outside of his remit, but no one had oversight over these guys, not even

Emerson. And when Emerson had approached top floor to ask for more information, he was shut down in a second. But one day Analytics and Subversion were called up to the sixth floor on an unscheduled meeting, and Emerson, Maynes and Gottfried were informed of this program the company had been working on for two years. No detailed information was given, they were simply told that testing was to be done on it and to find 'volunteers'. Finding volunteers nearly ended with the company being dragged to court. All the volunteers who were recruited for the program, thirteen of them, ended up dead and with their records expunged. Massive police cover-up. But they weren't the only dead; Emerson later pulled some sealed company files and found that Gulliver, the programmer, had been found in his flat with a bullet through his skull ten months into development. Ruled suicide, but who really knew. Three other developers who worked on the program were also found dead in suspicious circumstances. Only two survived, their names redacted from all records. Then there was the boy – a stroke of misfortune he'd got his hands on the program, but he couldn't be left to tell the tale. Now Zervas was the only one alive, to his knowledge, who'd been through the program and was alive to report on it. But god only knew if he'd be able to string a coherent sentence together when he next opened his eyes.

Emerson rounded the corner and stepped inside the open door of the recovery room. He stopped beside the bed. Zervas lay there still, eyes closed and lips slightly parted. Emerson picked up the folder that lay on a table next to Zervas's bed. His medical file. He flicked through it for a second, before closing it and dropping it on the table. It was far too dense and would tell him nothing he did not already know, or at least suspect.

Zervas was not awake, yet Emerson fancied he could make out some deep look of mourning on his face. No, not mourning – *repentance.* That was it. He looked like a man who'd come face to face with his maker and had settled some debts on his soul. Somehow, Emerson knew Zervas would never be able to do his job again.

'Sir…'

Emerson turned to see a nurse in the doorway. He nodded, stepped back from the bed and let her approach to check his vitals.

'He's stable?' Emerson asked. He glanced at her name tag. *Adeline.*

'Yes sir. Our EEG reading says he's emerged from the coma, but he hasn't come around yet. This is perfectly normal. It might be a day or two before he wakes up.'

'But it could be anytime…'

Adeline nodded. 'He might open his eyes at any second…' They both took a second to examine him, but Zervas lay supine. '…but who knows. The body makes its own decisions in such circumstances.'

'Of course.' Emerson sighed and pushed his hands into his pockets. He stared at the inert face of Zervas, not having anything useful to add. Adeline, noticing the drip bag almost empty, proceeded to replace it. 'I'll leave you alone. You'll contact me as soon as he awakes?'

'Of course, sir.'

Emerson turned and went out the door. He stopped at the glass for a second to take a last look at the unconscious patient. His forehead furrowed. Something troubled him, but he could not put a name to it.

*

Rodin left his office, locking it behind him and sliding the key into his jacket pocket. He glanced around the office, taking note of who was present. Then he exited the Security wing and went down the hall to the elevator. He got in, hitting the button for the basement sub-level, waiting for the doors to close before he took out his phone and turned it off, then slipped it back into his jacket pocket. He clasped his hands, the fingers of his right hand toying with the ring on the ring finger of his left. He looked at a dirty spot on the back of the elevator door and wondered how the cleaners had missed it. This was a well-kept building; the cleaning team was fastidious in its upkeep. He figured someone had sneezed and left a deposit on the back of the door; maybe it had only just happened.

He looked at the spot all the way to the sub-basement level. Just as the lift was slowing, unable to help himself, Rodin took a tissue from his pocket and wiped the spot from the back of the door.

The lift drew to a stop and the doors opened. Rodin stepped out, turning to drop the tissue into a bin next to the elevator. Then he proceeded down the hall.

At the end of the hall he opened a single, unmarked door and stepped inside. Inside, a woman sat at a desk in a plain, artificially lit room. The woman wore a plain gray dress suit. The table in front of her was devoid of anything save a clipboard and a pen.

The woman nodded. Rodin nodded. He stepped forward, picked up the pen, leaned in and signed his name on a sign-in sheet. He laid down the pen as the woman took the clipboard and turned it toward her, taking her own pen from the breast pocket of her suit jacket and signing her name next to his.

Rodin then proceeded around the desk, taking out his ID card. At the door, he pressed his ID against a scanner, which made no noise but to which the door promptly unlocked. Rodin went inside.

The room was dark but as Rodin made his way inside recessed lighting around the room came on, starting at the door and promptly working its way around the exterior, illuminating a long, low-ceilinged room filled with storage shelves end to end. On the shelves, files, and boxes filled with yet more files. Rodin stopped to look down the central aisle for a moment, before turning left and heading to the wall, turning right and walking about halfway down the room, where, at a desk, about half a dozen of which were stationed at intervals along the wall, he stooped and turned on a reading light, taking his ID from around his neck and setting it down, followed by his phone. He then took off his wedding ring and set it within the coiled lanyard of his ID. On the right side of the desk was a built-in console a little bigger than the size of a phone screen, dark, but when Rodin ran a finger across it it lit up. He took off his jacket and placed it over the back of the chair. Then he sat down. He placed his middle finger on the screen, unlocking it. Then he tapped the microphone icon on the screen, eliciting the soft chime of a bell and a steely female voice which said, 'Name and ID number please.'

Rodin stated his full name and ID number.

The voice said 'Thank you', followed by 'Function?'

Rodin said 'Update', to which the voice replied, 'Proceed'.

Rodin cleared his throat. 'Date, 1734 days beyond anomaly. Days to next purge, 137. Histories cleansed since last update – 7. Records resanctified under Protocol n17 – 184. Unavoidable erosion of historical data – 0.13 percent. Unavoidable recalibration of historical data – 2.42 percent. Database remains stable.' He paused, lightly stroking his forehead, taking a moment to dredge the necessary data from his mind. 'Probability of timely purge – 84.2 percent. Probability of timely anomaly – 91.7 percent.' Here he stopped, finishing with, 'Update complete.'

'Thank you,' the console answered in its lilting yet clinical voice. And then, 'Function?'

'Standby'.

'Yes.'

Rodin pushed back the chair and stood up. He turned and walked down the room, turning right into an aisle, additional recessed lighting coming on as he proceeded to the end where he crossed the central aisle to the other side. He stopped at a shelf tagged 'Staff Records 29Q-016', running his hand along the shelf until he came to a folder for 'Maynes, Maddox'. He pulled it out, stared at it for a second, then turned and went back the way he came, turning left this time and proceeding down the main aisle where he stopped at a central column. The column, around eight feet across and clad in bronze, ran from floor to ceiling. Ensconced in the column at chest height was a terminal, the screen black. Rodin stated his name and ID, causing the terminal to come to life.

'Function?'

Rodin looked at the cover of the folder in his hands once again. Cautiously, he opened the cover and looked at the first page. Name, date of birth, photo… etc. Rodin scrutinized the photo. A real mean-looking son of a bitch. No doubt about it. But like Rodin, a family man, with young children. Rodin flicked through the folder, stopping at a random page. Amid a sea of text, one name jumped out at him: *Selena Zervas.*

He snapped the folder shut and cleared his throat. 'Scan.'

Beneath the terminal display a large slot slid open, illuminated from the top by a red light. Maynes waited while a V-shaped cradle emerged forth from the back of the opening, then he placed the folder onto it, watched it retract, and waited as the scanner, by dint of the precise use of projected bursts of air to turn each page, proceeded to run through the file, digitizing each page in a fraction of a second. In a matter of moments, it was complete. The terminal spoke.

'Schedule for incineration?'

'Pending completion of current investigation…' Here he paused, taking a moment to adjust his tie. '…yes.'

The opening closed and the folder disappeared from view. Below the terminal screen another, smaller, slot opened. Rodin reached inside, and with finger and thumb extracted an optical disk about an inch in size. The slot closed. Rodin returned to the desk.

'Resume,' he said loudly upon sitting down in the seat.

The screen came back to life and prompted him to continue.

'Scan,' he instructed, and a small optical disk slot opened, into which Rodin placed the disk. The slot closed.

'Additional parameters?' the system prompted.

'System cross-reference database, general RQ-1. Security first, dissemination and escalatory fencing. Fallout and cataclysm. First responder, open protocol.' Here he paused, taking a breath. He sighed. 'Security additional, cross-reference exceptional Maynes, Maddox, with Zervas, Vangelis, with Gulliver, Ernest. Additional, program "Inferno", save top floor. Security clearance AQ Deprived.'

In what seemed like a matter of moments, the system confirmed.

'Scan complete.'

Rodin nodded. 'Security, deliver. Rodin alone.'

'Complete.'

Rodin picked up his wedding ring and slipped it onto his finger. He then took up his lanyard and put it over his neck.

'Function?' the console prompted.

'Terminate and sleep.'

'Thank you.'

The screen went black. Rodin stood up, taking up his jacket and putting it on. He cast his eyes over the desk, then turned and walked down the aisle. Behind him, the recessed lighting dimmed one after the other, until, arriving at the door, the room was dark once again.

8

'You seen this?'

Emerson held up the folder as he stepped into Rodin's office, closing the door behind him. Rodin nodded, closing the identical folder in his hands. Emerson took a quick glance through the windows, then turned back to Rodin before opening the folder.

'I mean, I dunno what the fuck to make of this... this is just off-the-charts crazy...' He flicked the page. 'Primary analysis of genetic material finds the remains of four different individuals. All male. One firearm – pistol – found, two knives, three different illicit substances...' Here he flicked forward again, pausing to grimace as if at a photo. 'Means of liquefaction, unknown.' He stopped reading to glance up at Rodin. Rodin stared at him grimly.

'*Liquefaction?* Four boys, *liquefied...*'

Emerson stared open-mouthed at Rodin as if for answers.

Rodin shook his head. 'I have no idea. None. In my whole career, I've never seen anything like it.'

Emerson shut the folder, pulled out a chair and sat down across the desk from Rodin. He scratched his chin and shook his head.

'You think it has something to do with Inferno?'

'I don't see how it can't. It has to be intimately tied up

in some way. There are things happening here that can't be explained without it.'

Emerson aggressively bit his lower lip. 'This fucking program.' He paused thoughtfully. 'Been causing problems ever since it was conceived.'

Rodin put down the folder and placed his hands on the desk. 'I need you to get me the files on Inferno. As head of Security, I can't ensure a complete investigation without them.'

Emerson placed his own hands on the desk, and leaned toward Rodin. 'You've asked me this already. And I've told you. I can't get those files.'

'You have the clearance.'

'*Yes I do*,' Emerson said, raising his voice a touch. 'But not for *those* files. Those files, for whatever fucking reason, are sealed. I can't touch them. I can't even get near 'em. I could go all the way to the sixth floor – and I have – and they still wouldn't let me get a look at them.'

Rodin shook his head imperceptibly.

'I know,' Emerson said. 'I'm in the fucking dark too...'

The phone on Rodin's desk rang. Rodin picked it up and put it to his ear, then held out the phone to Emerson, sitting back in his chair and swiveling a quarter turn away. Emerson raised the phone to his ear.

'Uh-huh...' A half minute's silence. 'Yes. Understood.'

He handed the receiver back to Rodin, who put it down.

'They're sending someone down.'

Rodin looked up from Maynes's file, which sat in his lap. 'Who?'

He shrugged. 'I dunno. Some "inter-company representative". That was all they said.'

Rodin took a moment to process this. 'That's a breach of protocol, surely. Security has the reins on all internal investigations.'

Emerson held up his hands. 'What can I do? It's the sixth floor. If they wanna send in a specialist, that's what they'll do.'

'A specialist...' Rodin closed the file and placed it on the desk. 'I presume you're talking about an interrogator?'

'What else would it be?' Emerson looked at Rodin for a long second before continuing. 'You know... there was that one time, what was it... about twelve years ago. You remember the Prentiss investigation? Naw, naw... that was before your time...'

Rodin butted in. 'I've seen the files.'

Emerson recollected his thoughts for a second. 'Yeah, we had this guy David Prentiss, a technician, who'd been smuggling in viruses and implanting them into company software. This was back in the days before we had complex scanning at all levels. He was doing it for almost fourteen months before he got caught. Whatever happened, and there are things about the case even I don't know – don't think everything is in the case file – top floor felt it urgent enough to override security protocols and intervene in the investigation. Seever, head of Security at the time, was livid. They sent down this... yeah, this creepy little fucker. Made the skin on the back of my neck crawl. I can't remember his name – I haven't seen him since. I bet it's the same bastard.'

'I don't like it.' Rodin picked up a pen and began to roll it in his fingers distractedly.

Emerson sighed. 'I don't suppose you do. But let me tell you – just let it go. It's above your clearance, and it's above mine.'

'How can I ensure security if my fucking clearance doesn't go all the way to the top?'

Emerson looked taken aback. 'In ten years, that's the first time I've heard you swear.'

Rodin cleared his throat, put a finger under his collar to pull it out from his neck. He looked embarrassed. 'Yeah, well, cutting me out of the circle renders my job somewhat redundant, doesn't it?'

Activity outside the office caused Rodin to look over Emerson's shoulder. He saw two men coming down the hall in his direction: one was du Pont, the other, a man he didn't know. Based on the tenseness of du Pont's gait, and the description of the interrogator provided earlier by Emerson, Rodin figured he knew who the man was.

'He's here.'

Emerson turned to glance over his shoulder, then turned back to Rodin gravely.

There was a knock at the door, then du Pont opened it and stuck his head inside.

'Sir, may we come in?'

Rodin nodded and stood up. Emerson was already on his feet. Du Pont came inside, followed by an insidious-looking man in black trousers and a black polo neck sweater. Thin and wiry, he had a sardonic, twisted air about him. He held a briefcase, the handle clasped in two hands in front of him. The man stopped in the middle of the floor without offering a hand. He looked at Emerson and nodded, glanced at Rodin before turning back to Emerson.

'I presume you had a call from upstairs?'

Emerson nodded. 'We did.'

The man glanced over his shoulder at du Pont. 'Your colleague will escort me presently to the interrogation room. I will be in there alone. Cameras are to be switched off, audio is to be switched off. I am not to be interrupted in the course of the interrogation. Any interruptions you feel strictly necessary are to go through sixth floor. They will contact me directly. Is all of this understood?'

He looked from Rodin, who nodded, to Emerson, who bit his lower lip.

'I've met you once before, haven't I?'

The man's lip turned up in a half smile. 'Yes you have.'

'Remind me of your name?'

'My name is Erdinger.'

'Erdinger... yeah.' Emerson glanced at the floor then back at Erdinger. 'We will accommodate all your requests. Consider it done.'

Erdinger nodded.

Emerson glanced down at the briefcase. 'You have everything you need? Can we get you anything?'

Erdinger shook his head. 'No. I'll get to my task now.' With a final look at the two men, he turned. Du Pont opened the door for Erdinger, who went out past him, then stopped and turned, waiting for du Pont to lead the way. Du Pont glanced at Rodin as he closed the door, one eyebrow lifting very slightly. Emerson and Rodin watched until du Pont and Erdinger had passed down the corridor and out of sight.

When they were gone, Emerson turned to Rodin.

'Any way you can get into the camera feed without alerting the system?'

'Yeah. By hacking it.'

Emerson grimaced. 'How risky?'

'If I don't trigger the firewall on entry, then none.'

'And if you do?'

Rodin smirked. 'I'm head of Security. I'm the first one who finds out. But there'll be a record of it, and sooner or later it'll be flagged.'

'Can it be traced to an internal source?'

'No. Not if I reroute it.'

Emerson stared at Rodin as his mind calibrated all the possibilities. His eyes had a kind of frantic intensity.

'Tell me we can do it…'

Calmly, Rodin opened a drawer in his desk and took out a hard-shell, military-style laptop case. He placed it on the desk and opened it, revealing a home-built portable system, with a screen secured to the inside of the unit and a keyboard embedded in the case.

'What the hell is that thing?' Emerson said as Rodin flicked it on.

'Built it myself. It'll run SSH over a decentralized network, all wrapped in multiple layers of encryption. The hack will be processed through so many independent nodes that it'll be untraceable, even if it does trigger the firewall.'

Emerson folded his arms. 'I don't know what the fuck any of that means.'

Rodin was now furiously punching commands into a terminal, multiple programs popping up on the screen at each moment. He worked with an intent suddenly furious and impenetrable. Emerson watched him at his task, the nail of his left thumb sawing anxiously between his two lower middle teeth.

Finally Rodin flicked his head to indicate a chair by the wall. Emerson grabbed it and pulled it up alongside the Security head. He peered at the screen.

'You in?'

'Yep.' He punched a button and the camera feed into Interrogation Room 2 flicked on. He turned the volume down, his eyes flicking up to scan the corridor outside his room.

'You trigger any alarms?'

'No. None that I've been alerted to anyway.'

Emerson glanced at him, the implications of that statement triggering some little below-the-surface alarms in Emerson's mind. Emerson shook his head at the thought.

The two men watched as, onscreen, Erdinger entered the room, stopping at the desk across which sat Maynes, hands cuffed to the desk in front of him. Erdinger laid the briefcase on the desk and stood for a moment with two hands on the chair. Maynes looked up at him.

'Is that fucker smirking?' Emerson said, looking at Maynes.

Rodin folded his arms. 'He looks like he knows something we don't.'

The two men sat, arms crossed, watching as Erdinger opened the briefcase, took out a folder and placed it on the desk, took out a small box and placed it on the desk too, then took out a pen. He closed the briefcase. Then he sat down.

'Hello Maynes,' Erdinger said. 'Do you remember me?'

Maynes didn't reply. He smiled.

'Creepy bastard,' Emerson muttered. 'You know, I never trusted him. Never. There was always something about him.

Something off. Not to mention that big fucking head of his... look at the size of it? Abnormal.'

'When did those two meet before?' Rodin asked.

Emerson shook his head. 'I didn't know they had.'

Rodin flexed his knuckles as he watched Erdinger open the folder and take out a series of photos, laying them on the table in front of Maynes.

'Investigation photos,' Emerson said.

Erdinger sat patiently as Maynes lowered his eyes to look at the pictures in front of him.

'I need to know what happened here,' Erdinger said simply, placing his two hands on the desk. 'What can you tell me about this scene?' He drew a hand across the table, indicating the photos.

Maynes stared at him hard, then licked his lips. There was a long, pregnant pause, then Maynes leaned in and spoke in hush but punctuated tones.

'A man came one day upon a bird in the road...' Emerson and Rodin leaned in, turning an ear to the screen. 'The bird was ailing, had a broken wing and was close to death. The man picked up the bird and took it home, and laid it in a small cot, and got to work, cleaning the bird and splinting the broken wing, and feeding it and nursing it. He even spoke gentle words to it in the evening to lull it to sleep...'

Emerson shared a confused glance with Rodin.

'After about six weeks the bird was back in good health, so the man took it into the garden and placed it in a tree. He waited, but the bird did not move. Each morning he came out into the garden, but the bird remained steadfast in its perch, only emitting a cawing each time the man came to check on it. When he went away, the bird cawed too, and went on like this from early morning until late at night. This went on for weeks. Finally the cawing of the bird became such that it drove the man crazy, and one morning he resolved to kill the bird, taking his shotgun and loading two shells and going out into the garden.' Maynes raised a finger at Erdinger.

'But this morning the bird did not caw. It stayed silent. And that silence was so deep, so profound, so totally endless in its intensity, that the man spiraled into a kind of black hole. Lifting the shotgun, he turned it around and put the barrel into his mouth and pulled the trigger.'

Maynes sat back in his chair. Erdinger sat in silence regarding him.

Emerson held his head in his hands in tense contemplation, glancing at Rodin once, eyes wide, before turning back to the screen.

Erdinger tilted his head as if the weight of what he'd just heard was still rolling around in his mind. 'Why are you telling me this?'

Erdinger lowered his eyes to Maynes's hands, laid flat on the table. Emerson leaned in as if to get a closer look.

'What the hell's that?' he whispered, jabbing a finger at the screen.

From their vantage over the security camera, it appeared Maynes's hands were leaking a black liquid, which was pooling on the table.

Rodin sat up straight in his chair, poised to jump up. As they watched, Maynes lifted his two hands from the desk, as if the cuffs restraining his wrists had suddenly fallen off. He rose up off his chair. Erdinger raised his face to look at Maynes, but did not speak. With the camera behind Erdinger, Emerson and Rodin couldn't read the expression on Erdinger's face.

Emerson's hands were on the armrests of his chair, as if about to propel himself forward.

'What's going on… why isn't he moving?'

Rodin reached for the desk phone, but Emerson clapped a hand on his wrist.

'If you call it in, they'll know we're watching.' Emerson looked him pointedly in the eye.

Rodin put the phone down and slipped a cell phone from his pocket. He dialed a number quickly as the two men watched Maynes walk around the table and position himself behind Erdinger. Maynes put his two hands on either side of Erdinger's head, his body blocking full visibility for the two watchers.

Emerson was up off his chair now. 'Goddamnit, we need to get someone in there…'

'Du Pont, where are you?' Rodin was up too and lifting his jacket from the back of the chair. 'Run by Interrogation Room 2, check everything's okay. Quickly.' Rodin pushed one arm into his jacket. 'I know what he said. Just do it. Stay on the line…'

Emerson, two fists pressed into the desk, watched the scene on the screen. 'I can't see… I can't see what he's doing.'

Rodin had his jacket on. 'We need to get down there…'

At that moment, they saw Maynes step away. He walked calmly around to the other side of the desk.

Emerson and Rodin stared open-mouthed, not moving.

Where Erdinger's head had been was now nothing more than a gelatinous black stump. Some kind of black jelly ran down over his back and shoulders and dripped to the floor.

Maynes sat down in his chair. He put his two hands on the desk and stared at the space where Erdinger's head had just been.

'Jesus fucking Christ, this is fucked…'

Emerson rushed toward the door. Rodin punched a few keystrokes on the keyboard, cutting access to the video feed. He shut the laptop and shoved it back in his desk, and hurried toward the open door.

In the corridor, he hurried after Emerson out of the Security wing and down the hall.

At the elevator, they bumped into Gottfried, who was just stepping out of the opening doors.

'Sir—'

Emerson held up a hand, rushing past him into the elevator. 'Not now – we got shit to deal with.'

'Sir—'

'Message Aline—'

'Sir!' Gottfried slapped a hand onto the elevator door, preventing it from closing. Emerson's eyes were wide with panic.

'Zervas has just woken up.'

Emerson clenched his hand into a fist and put it to his mouth.

9

I heard a beeping sound, at first far off, then more succinct. Then there was the sensation of brightness. Even with my eyes closed, I was aware of the light. But I couldn't open my eyes. It was like they were weighted, heavier than the universe. I became aware of my body and tried to move my limbs. They were heavy too, like concrete. I was suspended in a dense, oily heaviness.

Then I heard a voice.

I couldn't make out the words, like it was in some strange tongue. Or maybe just far away. When I tuned my ears to it, it became clearer, and I heard the sound of a woman. Not Celeste, someone else. I felt her hand on my body. Not in a sensual way, but in a prodding, clinical way. I became lucid, then. I realized where I was.

I still couldn't open my eyes but the heaviness started to lift from my body. The woman's hand was on my wrist, then my neck, then my temple. Her touch seemed to breathe life into my petrified limbs, and I was able to move the fingers of my left hand. She gauged my response; I felt an alarm in her touch. I moved my right hand. Then I moved my head.

A hot shudder ran from my head down through my limbs. As if my brain was the locus of some raging fire. A terrible thirst hit me, a dryness and a longing I'd never experienced.

I tried to force my eyes open, but they would not comply. The woman put her hand on my head and I heard her voice distinctly, very close to my ear.

'Easy now…'

She was holding my wrist again and I closed my hand around hers. She placed a cool, damp cloth on my forehead, then over my eyes, and after, as if she knew exactly what I needed, squeezed a few drops of water onto my lips.

I heard another figure bustle into the room, and when he spoke, I felt like I knew him but couldn't place who he was.

'He's awake?'

The woman replied. 'Almost.'

'I'll call upstairs.'

The male left.

I felt sensitive to my surroundings, like I could form a picture of them without my eyes, without even my ears. The more I came around, the stronger the picture I had of where I was.

The cool towel on my eyes soothed the violent sensation of light, and now I opened my eyes a crack. I saw out beneath the towel that I was in a hospital bed, or I figured, a bed in the medical wing of Vathos. The nurse dabbed more water onto my lips, and when I parted them, she let a few drops fall onto my tongue. Those few drops of water cause a series of sensations, first on my tongue, then in the rest of my body, and finally in my brain, that caused my entire being to light up, as if suddenly imbued with some magical element. I put my tongue out for more, but she made me wait, gently patting my chest and making soothing noises like you'd whisper to a baby. I suppose that's what I was, in some way – a newborn. A rushing horror tried to burst up from some dark place in my subconscious, but I fought it down, buried it away deep. Whatever it was I was waking from, I wasn't ready to face it just yet.

A few more drops of water alighted on my tongue.

'Do you want to try to open your eyes?' she said softly.

I nodded, and she took the damp towel from my face. I opened my eyes, squinting against the light. A nurse, bright white in her uniform, stood over me. Sensing movement from the other side, I turned my head, seeing a man step forward. I knew him. Squinting my eyes I focused on his face. Deen. He nodded gently, then looked up at the nurse. She took her cue and left.

Deen spoke softly. 'You can probably guess what's going to happen now, but I'll give you the heads-up, just in case. As soon as you're fully lucid you're going to be interrogated on your experiences of the last forty-eight hours. They're not going to let up – they'll drill you for whatever they can get. It won't be pleasant. It might take a day, it might take a week. Even a month. And then, when they feel they've gotten everything they can from you, they're going to kill you.' He turned to look at the monitors beeping above my head. 'If the interrogation doesn't kill you first.'

When I didn't reply, he said, 'Nod if you understand.'

I nodded. Then he patted me on the shoulder. 'You're made of strong stuff, I see that. But you're not going to survive this.' He turned to go, then stopped. 'A pity. You were a good agent. One of the best.'

He walked away. I closed my eyes.

The next sensation was one of being manhandled. Not the nurse, but of rough, unapologetic hands. I heard the voice of the nurse protesting, to no avail, as they hauled me out of bed.

'He can't even walk!' she shouted.

'We don't need him to,' one of the men replied.

Then I heard Emerson's voice. Unmistakable. 'Get him down to Interrogation. Room 1. Inject him with whatever you have to.'

The nurse protested, but I was dragged out of bed and thrown into a wheelchair.

Emerson waved a hand at the supply cupboard. 'Go get me some amphetamines or something. Anything.'

'Sir, I'm not auth—'

'I don't give a good goddamn!' Emerson shouted. 'Get me a needle filled with something spicy. I want him awake.'

The nurse complied, going to the cupboard. A pair of hands, a Security agent's, held me down in the chair.

Emerson fixed his eyes on me. 'You lucid?'

I nodded.

'Good.' He turned to the nurse. 'Here, get over here with that…'

She approached with the needle.

'Stick that in his arm. Hurry up…'

The nurse bent to my arm, cleaning a spot near the crook of my elbow. Then she stuck the needle in and sank the plunger. When she'd pulled out the needle, Emerson looked up at the Security agent.

'Go on. Get him downstairs.'

I sat in the wheelchair in the interrogation room, still in my medical gown. The white light burned my eyes, the sensation exacerbated by whatever they'd injected me with upstairs. Emerson came into the room, followed by Rodin, then Deen, who came in and set up his laptop on the desk in front of me. He didn't look at me.

Rodin leaned against the back wall and folded his arms nervously. Emerson paced the room, glancing up at me once as he waited for Deen to do whatever it was he was doing. When Deen was ready, he sat back in the chair, turning to Emerson and nodding. Emerson glanced over Deen's shoulder at the laptop. Then he turned his gaze on me, slowing his pace.

An uncomfortable tightness besieged every muscle in my body. I didn't know if it was the drugs or the days I'd spent unconscious. Or what had come before.

Emerson sighed then grimaced.

'Agent Zervas… you've just been subjected to a program that was buried in the company archives for a long time, something we never thought would see the light of day again. How you came to be exposed to this program, we won't get into. What we need to know, and quickly, is what you saw when you were in there.'

I lowered my eyes from his face; the white lights above his head were causing a burning in my skull.

'Can you lower the light in here?' I said.

'Agent Zervas,' Emerson said impatiently, 'forget the fucking lights. I need to know about your last forty-eight hours, and I need to know quickly.' I looked at Deen, who was scrutinizing me over the laptop screen. Emerson jabbed a finger at the screen. 'Bring up some of those images we were able to scrape from his mind.'

Deen punched a few keys, then tilted his head for some kind of acknowledgment from Emerson, who nodded. Deen turned the laptop to face me.

The image was of a lake of fire. My insides tightened. I closed my eyes against the image.

'Look at the fucking screen, Zervas. What is that – what can you tell me about that?'

I shook my head, pushing the image away. 'It's hazy… I can't put the whole picture together… it's like a bad dream you forget as soon as you wake up…'

Emerson came around next to me, placing his two hands on the desk. He leaned his face in close to mine. The stench of stale coffee hit me. Another smell, too – whiskey, from the night before.

Emerson lowered his voice, still thick with menace. 'I need you to wake up outta that bad dream and tell us what the fuck happened down there.' He jabbed a finger into the top of my skull. 'We got some shit happening we can't explain, and we're going to get answers out of you even if it means cutting you open. So get to remembering, and quick.'

Deen punched the keyboard, bringing up another image. I looked at it, feeling a cold horror in my chest. It was blurry, hazy, but I knew exactly what it was.

'What the fuck is that?' Emerson quizzed. '*Who* the fuck is that?'

I raised my face to the ceiling, eyes closed, and breathed. Then I returned my gaze to the image. 'That's me.'

'That's you?' Emerson looked at Deen, then at Rodin. 'What do you mean it's you? What's going on here, are you some kind of fucking angel or what?'

'I was tortured.'

'Tortured… by who?'

I shook my head. 'It's difficult to explain—'

'Try, damnit!'

Emerson's face was red. He was angry. But more than that… he was scared. I saw fear in his eyes. He had no idea what he was dealing with, and he didn't like it.

'Did you see Maynes when you were down there? We know he was in there with you – did you see him?'

I looked at the torture picture. 'Yeah.'

Emerson cast a glance at Rodin before turning back to me. 'Well? What happened? What was he doing?'

'Maynes was there,' I repeated. 'Except he wasn't really Maynes. He was…'

I petered off, staving off a flood of memories that threatened to annihilate me.

'He was what, damnit?' Emerson had his hands on his hips, impatient for an answer.

'He was… Satan.'

The three men froze. No one spoke. A chill seized the room.

Two hours later, I was dragged into a holding cell. One of Rodin's Security underlings pushed me onto a cot, then undid the handcuffs around my wrists.

The room was sparse, walls white. Same white lighting, but not as bright as the interrogation room. A toilet and a sink.

'I'm hungry,' I said, rubbing my wrists.

The Security grunt left, leaving only Rodin.

'Food will be sent in.'

He glanced at the camera in the corner of the room. I followed his gaze.

'Don't worry,' I said, stretching my legs. 'I'm not going to kill myself.'

Rodin nodded noncommittally. 'Probably doesn't matter.' He regarded me for a moment. 'Make yourself comfortable.'

Then he turned and went to the door. He went out and closed it without another look over his shoulder. I heard his footfall progress down the hall.

I looked around at the four walls. This was it. This was the last room I'd ever know. The last cot I'd lie in. A grim emptiness hit me. I swung my legs up and lay back on the cot, putting my arm over my eyes. All I wanted was for them to dim the fucking lights.

Later, lulling me from the clutches of undefined nightmares, whispers came to me. They spoke to me through the darkness of my dreams, laying a whole other skein of terror over the machinations of my subconscious, propelling me into yet greater unease, until my eyes opened to the dark of the room.

In the corner of the room, an LED on the camera blinked. Then I heard the whisper again, and I realized it wasn't a projection of my dreams. It was real.

'Zervas…'

It came from nearby, through a wall somewhere. Through a vent. Stole in and made my skin crawl.

'Zerrrvvas…'

It was Maynes. Or almost him. Behind it was the unmistakable drawl of the man in the silver suit. But somewhere within that terrible intonation, Maynes lurked.

'I'm here, right here. Right on the other side of the wall. Can you feel me? Here… put your hand to the wall, I'll make you feel me. I'll put myself inside you…'

A burning took hold in my stomach, and it made its way somehow into my limbs, via my veins or my nervous system, I don't know, but I started to shudder.

'Feel it? Feel me inside you? I know you can, you fucker. I know you feel me in every cell of your body.'

I sat up in the dark, put my feet on the cold floor. The sliding panel over the small window on the door was closed. The only light was a faint sliver running along the bottom of the door. There were no sounds from the hall outside.

'*Zervas…*'

The hairs on the back of my neck stood up, and a tremor shook my body.

'*You know it, don't you? Know I'm a part of you now. You know that whether you run or hide, live or die, I'll always be a part of you. You feel it in your balls, your belly, your soul… I am a part of you. Thus I have made you holy…*'

I felt frozen in place. Like I couldn't move. I looked toward the door, looking for someone to come in, to stop the cold whispers assailing me. No one was coming. It was just me. And him.

'*In you, around you, on you… Let's be together, Zervas. You and me. Let us make each other whole…*'

I felt a cold sensation around my feet. Dropping my eyes to the floor, I squinted. A thick black sludge was pooling around my feet. Momentarily, I couldn't process it, as if part of my nightmares had somehow crept into waking life and was lingering somewhere between the two states. The pool grew bigger, and my feet grew colder.

I tried to stand up, but my body wouldn't obey my urges.

'*That's it, Zervas, let yourself go. Let us be joined, each to the other. Let me subsume you…*'

Mustering my will, I pushed myself to my feet, stepping out of the black sludge and throwing up the cot attached to the wall. A thick stream of black sludge was pouring out of the vent in the wall below the cot.

I turned my face to the door, my head ringing. I screamed: 'HE'S HERE!'

The black sludge began to snake over my feet and up my ankles.

I ran at the door and smacked it with my fists.

'HE'S HERE! HE'S COME BACK!'

CONTINUE WITH THE FINAL PART...

1. Cerebrum

Subconscious torture for political and corporate subversion. That's the trade of Vathos—creeping into a target's dreams to force the shady ends of their clients. It's dirty business.

Vangelis Zervas is one of their Subversion agents and makes a living inflicting pain on people in their sleep. A recipient of the most stringent training and a man of few qualms, he'll do whatever it takes to get the job done. But when a series of events calls his dedication into question, strange things begin to happen when he infiltrates the dreams of his targets. Soon he's asking himself—is it he in the mark's head, or is someone else in his?

A no-holds-barred dystopian horror that will put your teeth on edge.

2. Acolyte

Caleb, a young school dropout, robs an apartment one night with his petty-criminal friend, Vince. Finding an expensive and rare piece of computer hardware, he pockets it, oblivious to its power and purpose. The boy plugs himself into the new device, unaware that the program inside it is a diabolical piece of software, one which almost kills him. But those who created the program do not want it out in the world and will do anything to retrieve it, including killing anyone in whose possession it is found. Caleb may find that by taking the device he has unwittingly unleashed forces that will consume all he knows and loves.

3. Chimera

Following the murder of her young son, Celeste goes all in with a group of co-conspirators to infiltrate Vathos, the company she believes responsible for the death of her child. The faction make tentative contact with Vangelis Zervas, hoping he will help them penetrate the Vathos servers so they may gather evidence to bring the company down. Despite the nature of his ruthless and horrific work, Vangelis may have his own misgivings with the company. But is it enough for him to turn on Vathos?

In the end, he may have only one choice: Hell or death.

4. Inferno

After a penetration operation on the Vathos servers goes awry, Celeste and Vangelis Zervas are cast into the Vathos mainframe following a possible sabotage operation from within the company. The pair are drawn into the 'Inferno' program, a devious piece of software long held in the companies archives, the program a digitalized recreation of Hell itself. Celeste and Zervas are pursued by Maynes, who, having discovered that the agent has gone rogue, is hell-bent on retribution. But no one gets through Inferno unscathed. Evil begets evil, and soon Celeste and Zervas will come face to face with something far darker, and far more sinister than Maynes.

5. Diablo

Within every man is a devil. There is only one Satan.

Vangelis Zervas has just been subjected to the most insidious psychological program ever invented by man. He comes out of it in a coma, sequestered in the Medical wing at Vathos systems. Maddox Maynes, his supervising officer, has also returned from their encounter in 'Inferno', still conscious but carrying something deeply sinister within him. The reverberations of the program are carried from the virtual into the real, as Vathos is shaken from within by the greatest enemy it will ever face. This is the beginning of the end.

Little Swine

A small basement cell. A dirty bed. A chair.

These are the confines of Little Swine's world. Prisoner of Momma and subject to the tortures of Boy, her life is a living hell.

Momma has a plan. Momma wants a baby that she may redeem the sins of her past. This is Little Swine's purpose. And when Momma has what she wants, Little Swine will be discarded.

But violence begets violence and blood begets blood, and many will die before the devil has his quota. One can never underestimate the power of retribution.

The Cottage

Men are men until they encounter evil. And after, they are compelled to do evil itself.

Turning their backs on New York, John and Katie Mears purchase their dream home in colonial Connecticut, the place they hope to raise their firstborn and build life as a family. But the cradle of the American nation has a haunting past, and they find themselves swallowed by a dark history, one of blood and anguish, a specter of the country's painful birth in the slaughter of pilgrim times. The dark crucible of the nation is yet manifest. Blood debt is eternal, and sooner or later history calls for retribution. It is the blood of innocents that pays for the sins of the father.

MEAT

In the murky wake of the financial crisis a string of establishments pop up across Europe catering to a hedonistic underground, its clientele beholden to a strange, hallucinatory meat. Stoked by the fleshy and charismatic Hugo and fuelled by voracious consumption of ecstasy, the craze spreads from the heart of Europe all the way to the Mediterranean, where in Athens the financial elite begin to turn on each other. Murder, barbecue and apocalyptic raving ensues, culminating in the most savage party Mykonos has ever seen. Follow the story to its destructive end, where consumption eats itself alive.

NOTES FROM A CANNIBALIST

1847. Assuming the identity of a dead Jesuit priest, a survivor of the famine in Ireland travels to South America where he is tasked with rebuilding the missions among the natives. Inducted into local life, Father James Carmichael finds love with a native woman and becomes acquainted with the ways of the Guaraní, discovering ayahuasca and ritualism. In a battle with his own gods and demons, the priest fights for the life he envisions, his own self the ultimate stake of the struggle. Worlds are shattered, realities crumbled, lives destroyed. His soul victim to the crucible of the New World, what is tempered in the chaos will be outside his control.

A WHORE'S SONG

Hidden away in the backstreets of Amsterdam is a secretive whorehouse, open only to those in the know, where torture, pain and extreme sexual sport are the vehicle to understanding and self-knowledge. Run by the obscure Madame Zhu, the establishment is a magnet to the city's elite and mad soul-seekers alike. Two lives collide in a chaotic downward spiral brought about by psychoactives and sexual torture when, over the course of a day, a whore recounts her life as a destroyer of egos and one man is forced to face his deepest demons. Cast out into the far reaches of his mind, will he make it back from the other side?

In a world where the weak become prey and strength means brutality, living may come at the cost of dying first.

The Book of God

God isn't dead. He's just a bit mental...

Indignant at his corrupt and ignominious creation, God sits and stews in his treehouse outside the small town of Brawl. His only companion and sole remaining attendant, a withered and tortured scribe, chronicles the Lord's descent into madness as he struggles to collect all the lost souls which have escaped his records and further addled the Lord's already woolly mind. But when the Scribe is forced to hire a maid to care for the Almighty, the introduction of a buxom woman into God's life brings chaos in its wake. And what's more, the maid has an innocent and attractive young daughter...

Suffering rejection, humiliation and loathing of humankind, God seeks a way to bring back Christ and trigger the Apocalypse. The only thing standing in his way? God's old harpy of a mother...

The Jaguar

1849. Salome Azul, daughter of a powerful politician, flees Buenos Aires at the height of the Argentinian civil war. In London she enlists the help of Irishman Sean Ryan to open The Nightingale, a high-class brothel and opium den that will be used to entrap and blackmail London's political elite.

In doing so she will make enemies. What's more, Ms. Azul has carried her own demons from Argentina, and it is these that will prove her most relentless foe. In order to survive, she must eliminate all weakness from her character. Doing so may mean cutting away all she cherishes most.

In the pursuit of power, unrelenting sacrifice is what decides who lives and dies.

WORKS OF TRANSLATION BY ULTAN BANAN

Pietro Aretino's Dialogues

Nanna has been a nun. She's been a wife. She has also been a courtesan. And now, as her daughter turns sixteen, she must decide how to advise on her path in life. On what route should she send young Pippa?

Bawdy, filthy, hilarious and uproarious, listen to Nanna regale her friend Antonia with scandalous tales—tales of seduction, blasphemy, lies, dishonesty, thievery, nastiness, cruelty and treachery—in an attempt to decide on what course to set her daughter: should she be a nun, a wife or a whore?

Ultan Banan started writing as a way of getting his head straight, discovering in the process that staying busy is the only way to stop oneself going insane. He devotes what time he can to writing, doing his best to avoid gainful employment by increasingly creative means. He lives on the move but dreams of a small cottage on a foul and inhospitable coast somewhere. Currently in Scotland.

Latest news at
ultanbanan.com

Substack:
ultanbanan.substack.com

Twitter:
twitter.com/ultanbanan

www.ingramcontent.com/pod-product-compliance
Lightning Source LLC
Chambersburg PA
CBHW051712180726
48283CB00004B/1313